SAVAGE REVENGE

Sawyer blinked a few times. "You're here too? Well, isn't this something? All my friends are showing up. How did you hear a[illegible]e and my pr[illegible]ts? About the murd[illegible] nearly killed me. I'[illegible]

Nate darted between his friend and the animals. "Hold on, Jeremiah," he said kindly, putting a hand on the man's chest. "You're not going anywhere right this minute. You need food; you need some sleep. And we have to talk."

Sawyer's features clouded and his spine went rigid. "Get out of my way, Nate. I can't afford any more delays. Those butchers have a lot to answer for."

"You're not leaving," Nate said.

It was plain as the nose on his face that his friend was extremely upset, so Nate expected to get an argument. What he didn't expect was for Sawyer to haul off and take a swing at him.

"No!" Jeremiah wailed. "You have to let me go! Those bastards have to pay!"

The *Wilderness* series published by *Leisure Books:*

 # 1: KING OF THE MOUNTAIN
 # 2: LURE OF THE WILD
 # 3: SAVAGE RENDEZVOUS
 # 4: BLOOD FURY
 # 5: TOMAHAWK REVENGE
 # 6: BLACK POWDER JUSTICE
 # 7: VENGEANCE TRAIL
 # 8: DEATH HUNT
 # 9: MOUNTAIN DEVIL
#10: BLACKFOOT MASSACRE
#11: NORTHWEST PASSAGE
#12: APACHE BLOOD
#13: MOUNTAIN MANHUNT
#14: TENDERFOOT
#15: WINTERKILL
#16: BLOOD TRUCE
#17: TRAPPER'S BLOOD
#18: MOUNTAIN CAT
#19: IRON WARRIOR

GIANT SPECIAL EDITIONS:

HAWKEN FURY
SEASON OF THE WARRIOR
PRAIRIE BLOOD

20

WILDERNESS

Wolf Pack

David Thompson

LEISURE BOOKS  NEW YORK CITY

To Judy, Joshua, and Shane

A LEISURE BOOK®

January 1995

Published by

Dorchester Publishing Co., Inc.
276 Fifth Avenue
New York, NY 10001

Printed in the United States of America.

Chapter One

Jeremiah Sawyer had lived in the Rocky Mountains for over five years. He knew them as well as he knew the palms of his hands. The ways of the wild beasts, the ways of the various Indians tribes—they were all familiar to him.

So when a red hawk soaring high to the southeast uttered a piercing cry, Jeremiah looked up from the snare he was in the act of setting along a rabbit run.

Hawks made different sounds. There were the low whistlelike cries made by mating pairs as they whirled in aerial ballet. There were the occasional throaty cries of challenge issued by males. And there were those piercing cries of warning such as Jeremiah had just heard.

Straightening, the burly free trapper scanned the adjacent mountain slopes. He saw a few mule deer to the south, several mountain sheep on the craggy heights to the north. Other than the hawk, which had sailed to the east over the entrance to Jeremiah's little valley, nothing else moved.

Jeremiah sank to one knee to finish the snare, then froze, deeply troubled. He'd learned to rely on his gut instincts during his years of wilderness living, and his intuition was telling him to get back to his lodge as quickly as possible. Scooping up his rifle, he adjusted his possibles bag under his left arm and took off at a trot.

The hawk might have seen riders coming, Jeremiah reflected. Visitors were rare to the remote valley he called home. Every now and then some of his wife's people, the Crows, would stop by. And every blue moon another mountain man would show up to share a drink or three and a plug of chaw.

There was another, more disturbing possibility.

Jeremiah's sanctuary was nestled along the border of Crow country. To the south lived Utes, perennial enemies of the Crows. To the east lived Arapahoes and Cheyennes, who sometimes raided deep into Crow land. And well to the north lived the Blackfeet, who were at war with all tribes not belonging to their confederacy.

Jeremiah had long lived with a secret dread of the valley being found by an enemy war party. He had picked the isolated site because it was so far off the beaten path that getting into a racket with hostiles was unlikely. But a man never knew when fate would rear its ugly head.

The sun hung high in the afternoon sky. Soon, Jeremiah knew, Yellow Flower would begin making supper. She and the girls had spent the morning gathering berries and roots, and the last Jeremiah had seen them, they had been pounding stakes into the ground so they could stretch out the hide of a black bear he had killed the day before and scrape the hide clean of tissue and hair.

If anything ever happened to them, Jeremiah did not know what he would do with himself. Before he met Yellow Flower, he had been a wanderer and a bit of a rake. Now, she was his anchor, the source of the greatest happiness he had ever known—a happiness so deep and so intense that he gave thanks every day for the blessing of her love. Together with his daughters, she gave his life meaning.

Suddenly the air was rent by a faint scream, punctuated by a gunshot.

Fear rippled down Jeremiah's spine. He poured on the speed, running as fast as his legs would fly. In his mind's eye he imagined his family being set upon by Blackfeet or Bloods. Yellow Flower was fearless and a fair shot, but she was no match for a war party of seasoned warriors.

The high grass lashed Jeremiah's legs. He could see the stand of pines in which the lodge was located, but as yet was unable to catch a glimpse of the clearing where it stood. His possibles bag and ammo pouch slapped against his chest as he ran, and he had to keep one hand on his pistol or risk having it slip out from under his belt.

Jeremiah was within 50 yards of his goal when another shot rang out. He thought he heard gruff laughter, but couldn't be sure.

Convinced hostiles were definitely to blame, Jeremiah slowed as he neared the trees. It would do his loved ones no good if he were to blunder in among his enemies and be slain outright.

He cocked his rifle when he entered the pines. Gliding from trunk to trunk, Jeremiah strained his ears to catch more sounds, but heard only a vague rustling. Then he saw the lodge, awash in a beam of sunlight, and in front of it were seven horses he had never seen before.

Jeremiah halted behind the last trunk to survey the clearing. A thin tendril of smoke wafted from the top of the lodge, as it always did when Yellow Flower cooked a meal. The flap hung open. As he watched, a shadow flitted across the opening.

The next moment a tall man emerged.

To say that Jeremiah was surprised would be an understatement. The visitor was a fellow trapper, a company man, an employee of the Rocky Mountain Fur Company. Jeremiah had run into him at the last rendezvous. Holding his rifle level, Jeremiah boldly strode into the open. "Lassiter?"

The tall man turned, a smile creasing his rugged features. "So there you are. I was wondering where you had gotten to, hos. After I came all this way just to see you, I was afeared you were off on a gallivant and wouldn't be back for weeks."

"I never leave my family except during trapping season," Jeremiah said. He glanced at the lodge, then at the horses. "Who are you with? Where are the others? What was all the shooting about? I thought I heard a scream."

"My, my, aren't you a bundle of questions?" Lassiter said. He sat down on an old stump and rested his rifle across his thighs. "Have a seat, friend. We have some talking to do."

"I'd rather check on my family first," Jeremiah

said, moving toward the tepee.

Lassiter made a clucking sound. "Maybe your ears are plugged full of wax. I want to palaver and I want to do it right this minute."

Jeremiah didn't care for the man's tone. "I'll do as I damn well please, thank you. You can just hold your horses a minute or two." At the opening he lowered his rifle, bent at the waist, and went to enter. The next moment he found himself staring down the barrel of a gun held by a huge man in greasy buckskins.

"I'd do as Lassiter says, mister, were I you."

Caught flat footed, Jeremiah backed away, careful not to elevate his rifle. The huge man squeezed through the gap, revealing a shock of black hair as greasy as his clothes.

"Don't plug him, Bear," Lassiter said. "We need him alive."

From out of the pines came more strangers, five in all. Three wore garb typical of mountaineers. One appeared to be a half-breed. The last, incredibly, was a Blood Indian.

"What the hell is going on here?" Jeremiah demanded. "Where's my family?"

"You'll see them soon enough," Lassiter said smugly. "Provided you cooperate with us, hos."

"Cooperate?" Jeremiah said. He could not help but notice that the other men had fanned out to form a ring around him. He was completely hemmed in and dared not lift a finger or he would be instantly cut down.

Lassiter scratched the stubble on his chin. "Let me explain, Sawyer. At the last rendezvous I heard tell that you always trade a goodly number of your plews for gold coins. The word is that you have a big stash cached somewhere. I want them."

The audacity of the man would have been laughable if not for his six menacing companions. Jeremiah tried a bluff. "I don't know what in the hell you're flapping your gums about. If I had a stash of gold, I wouldn't be living in the middle of nowhere in a buffalo-hide lodge. I'd be back in the States, set up proper in a fancy mansion with servants at my beck and call."

A cruel grin creased Lassiter's mouth. "I didn't say that you were as rich as old King Midas. The story is that you have a few thousand socked away, is all."

"And who fed you this lie?" Jeremiah said. "Someone three sheets to the wind, I reckon."

"His name doesn't matter," Lassiter said. "All that need concern you is giving us the money. Do it now and spare yourself a heap of grief."

"You just waltz in here and steal me blind, is that it?"

"More or less."

Jeremiah flushed with anger when several of the men snickered at his expense. "Are all of you company men? What do you think will happen when your employers find out what you've been up to?"

"Really, Sawyer. Are you dunderhead enough to think that I still work for the Rocky Mountain Fur Company?" Lassiter shook his head. "It wasn't for me. Long hours and working like a dog for a pittance. No thanks. I've found a better way."

"You've turned to robbery."

"Among other things."

The sinister tone the man used sparked raw

fear in Jeremiah. Not for himself, but for those he cared for most. Shifting, he tried to peer into the lodge but he was at the wrong angle.

"Drop the rifle," Lassiter said abruptly. No sooner were the words out of his mouth than the other five trained their weapons on Jeremiah's chest. "And do it nice and slow unless you're partial to the notion of being turned into a sieve."

Reluctantly, Jeremiah obeyed. He was so furious he could barely think straight. All he wanted was to get his hands around the bastard's throat.

"That's being smart," Lassiter said. "Now tell us where we can find this gold of yours?"

Without hesitation Jeremiah squared his shoulders and said, "I don't have any."

"Think again. Believe me when I say you don't want us to pry the information from your lips."

"I'd like to see you try," Jeremiah said, poised to draw the flintlock if a single one of them came toward him. He would rather die fighting for his life than submit meekly like a weakling.

"Suit yourself," Lassiter said, and he made a gesture with his right hand.

Jeremiah was tensed to strike. Years of wilderness living had turned his body into iron whipcord, and he was certain he could draw and fire before any of the cutthroats reached him. He glanced from one to the other. The one called Bear took a step toward him and Jeremiah whirled, his hand clawing for the polished butt of a smooth-bore pistol. Too late he realized it was a ploy, a trick to divert his attention.

Like a pair of striking serpents, the Blood and the half-breed pounced, closing from different directions as once. Out of the corners of his eyes Jeremiah saw them coming and tried to turn to confront them but they were on him in an instant. Steely fingers seized his. He winced as his arms were savagely wrenched behind his back. A moccasin flicked out and caught him across the shin. The next thing he knew, he was on his knees in front of a smirking Lassiter.

"Some folks just have to learn the facts of life the hard way."

"Go to hell!"

Lassiter slowly rose, his lean form resembling that of a rattler rearing to strike. "I'm afraid you'll be suffering the fires of damnation long before I will. For the last time, Sawyer, where's your gold?"

Jeremiah preferred to die than reveal the secret. But he had his wife and daughters to think of. Rather than keep up the pretense, he asked bluntly, "What about my family? If I tell you, will you let them go?"

Some of the ruffians laughed.

"You still haven't seen the light, have you?" Lassiter said. "You're going to tell us one way or the other. As for your family, they're not worth fretting yourself over."

The sadistic gleam in the tall man's eyes caused an icy knot to form in Jeremiah's breast. "What do you mean?"

"Show him, boys."

Bear came over and grabbed hold of Jeremiah's hair. The Blood and the breed held onto his arms. Between the three of them, they hauled Jeremiah over to the lodge and Bear pushed his head low enough for him to see the interior clearly.

At the sight of the three bodies, each lying in a

spreading pool of blood, Jeremiah was overcome by dizziness and his limbs turned to mush. Bitter bile filled his mouth. It was all he could do to catch a breath.

Yellow Flower was naked, lying on her side by the fire she had started. Her torn beaded dress lay nearby. There was a bullet hole in her left breast.

The two girls were at opposite sides of the tepee. The oldest had been knifed, slit open from navel to chin. The youngest had been shot in the stomach. Both girls, mercifully, were clothed.

Harsh, grating mirth shattered Jeremiah's daze and brought him back to the land of the living. A potent rage gripped him, rage such as he had never known, and without thinking, he twisted and slammed his right foot into Bear's left knee even as he whipped the Blood into the breed.

Jeremiah found himself free. He could have turned, wrested a gun from one of them, and tried to slay Lassiter before the rest made wolf meat of him. But he was too canny for that. He wanted revenge on all of them. So the moment they let go, he streaked around the lodge and into the trees while to his rear Lassiter bellowed.

"After him, you jackasses! Don't let him get away!"

Limbs snatched at Jeremiah's face and hands. He didn't care. Blood flecked his cheeks and wrists. It didn't matter. In all the world only his vengeance mattered.

Then the lead started to fly.

Chapter Two

Nathaniel King was on his way home after a successful hunt. Packed on the three extra horses he had brought along were the remains of an elk he had picked off at 200 yards. He was rightfully proud of the shot, made in heavy timber when the bull was on the move. Few men could have made it.

Nate was a member of the trapping fraternity, a man who caught and sold his own hides rather than work for a fur company.

Typical of his hardy kind, Nate wore buckskins and moccasins. A Hawken rested across his saddle. A pair of matching flintlocks adorned his waist, as well as a long butcher knife and a tomahawk. He was armed for bear, as the saying went, and with good reason.

A lone white man never knew when he might wind up beset by Indians or animals determined to deprive him of his life. The rate at which trappers perished was fearsome. In any given year, out of scores who ventured into the wild to make their fortune laying traps for beaver, a quarter of them fell victim to the random perils so common in the mountains.

Only the toughest survived for more than two or three seasons. Exceptional were those who lasted longer, men like Nate King, men who became as hard as their surroundings.

On this day Nate rode along a spine connecting two high country slopes. He had chosen the high lines so he could keep his eyes skinned for movement below. It paid for a man to have eyes like an eagle, as his mentor Shakespeare McNair so often said.

Thinking of McNair brought a smile to the big man's face. It had been a spell since last he saw his best friend, so a visit was long overdue. It would do their wives good to get together, and Nate's kids never tired of the antics of their Uncle Shakespeare.

The black stallion that Nate rode pricked its ears and swung its head to the west. Nate looked and immediately reined up.

Crossing the next valley were four riders. At that distance it was impossible to note details. Nate recognized them as Indians though and drew into the shadows to keep from being seen.

They might be friendly Shoshones, Nate's adopted tribe. They might even be Crows. But it had been Nate's hard experience never to take anything for granted. The warriors might just as well be unfriendly and he didn't care to tangle with them if it could be avoided.

Nate observed them carefully. They rode in single file, Indian fashion, two on pintos, another on a bay, the last on a sorrel. Their angle of travel would take them south of the spine and put them between him and home.

Only when the quartet had vanished into thick timber did Nate ride from cover and descend the far side of the spine, threading among tightly packed firs and deadfalls. At the bottom he swung to the south, holding the stallion to a walk. The three packhorses plodded along wearily, no doubt as anxious to reach their small corral as he was to reach his cabin.

Often Nate stopped to look and listen. The stock of the .60-caliber Hawken rested on his right thigh. Made by the master craftsmen Jacob and Samuel Hawken of St. Louis, Hawkens were rapidly gaining a reputation as the most reliable guns ever made. Nate's sported a smooth 34-inch octagonal barrel, a crescent-shaped butt plate, low sights, and a percussion lock.

His pistols were also works of quality. Single-shot .55-caliber flintlocks, they were almost as powerful as the Hawken at short range.

All three were vastly superior to the trade guns given Indians. Fusees, as they were called, often blew apart or misfired or broke readily. They were of such poor workmanship that most Indians preferred to rely on their bows and arrows rather than the white man's weapon of choice.

Crowning Nate's shock of black hair was a beaver hat. A Mackinaw coat lay draped over the back of his saddle. He was glad it was there and not on his person. A red coat stood out in a green forest like the proverbial sore thumb.

The woodland thinned. Far ahead figures moved. Nate halted, his eyes narrowing against the glare of the high sun. The Indians were there, all right, heading due south now, the same direction he had to take.

"Damn," Nate said to himself and pulled in behind a briar patch. He had a choice to make. Should he play it safe, camp there until morning, and then go on? Or should he try to swing around ahead of them?

As if he truly had much of a choice. The disturbing fact was that he happened to be less than ten miles from the cabin. If the warriors kept on as they were going, they'd probably get there before nightfall.

Nate wished Shakespeare was along. The two of them had licked their weight in hostiles more times than he cared to count. As it was, he would have to rely on a sizable portion of pure luck if he hoped to save his family.

Prodding the stallion with his heels, Nate angled to the left, moving parallel to the warriors. Mentally he reviewed the lay of the land in front of them—countryside he had traveled through so often he could ride across it at a full gallop in the dead of a moonless night and avoid every obstacle in his path.

Nate marked the position of the sun, then turned his attention to the ridge ahead. That ridge overlooked the domain he had claimed as his own, a verdant valley three times the size of most, watered by a lake rife with fish and fowl, a virtual paradise.

Presently Nate came to a hillock. Stopping shy of the crest, he dismounted, ground hitched the stallion, and crept to the top. From his vantage point he saw the warriors plainly. His mouth became a thin slit and his eyes as flinty as quartz.

They were Utes.

Like the Blackfeet, Piegans, and Bloods to the north, the Utes had made no secret of their dislike for whites. They regarded trappers as invaders and either ran off or slew every mountain man they found in their territory.

Nate's valley happened to be at the northern limit of the Ute range. Years ago, when Nate first settled there, the Utes had made annual raids in an effort to drive him off. They had failed.

It was doubtful the four warriors were part of a war party; none were painted for war. Nate figured it was a hunting party, maybe younger warriors eager to count coup who had decided to test the mettle of the white devil they had heard so much about from older men.

Nate had to stop them before they reached his valley. And since he would find no better spot to make a stand, he pressed the Hawken to his shoulder and fixed a bead on the back of the last warrior. It would be an easy shot. The Ute would never know what hit him.

But Nate lowered the Hawken and stood. He had never been a backshooter by nature, a weakness some of the other free trappers had mocked him for having. To them, shooting an enemy in the chest or between the shoulder blades was all the same. As one voyager from Canada had so succinctly put it, "A dead enemy is a dead enemy. *C'est la guerre, mon ami.*"

Swallowing hard, Nate planted both feet, made

sure his ammo pouch and powder horn hung loosely across his chest, and cupped a hand to his mouth. From his lips issued the lusty war whoop of his adopted people, the Shoshones.

The Utes wheeled their mounts and sat staring at him. Evidently suspecting a trick, they made no move to come toward him.

Nate tensed, ready to leap for cover when they charged. They were just out of bow range. By the time they got close enough, he would be flat on his stomach, picking them off as fast as he could.

The huskiest of the warriors broke ranks, riding slowly forward, his bow slung across his back, a lance held low at his side. He acted calmly, as if he were riding into his own village.

Keeping one eye on the others, Nate cradled the Hawken in the crook of his left elbow. He wouldn't put it past the Utes to try a trick of their own.

The warrior drew near enough for Nate to see the man's features clearly, and Nate allowed himself to relax. Grinning, he strode to the bottom of the hillock and used sign language to say, "It has been many moons, Two Owls."

The Ute chief whom Nate had befriended years ago reined up and smiled in genuine friendship. "Too many moons, my brother. Question. Your family is well?"

"And growing. I have a girl now."

"Does your son follow in your footsteps?"

"He tries."

"Then he will grow to be a man of honor, as is his father." Two Owls turned somber. "Question, Grizzly Killer," he signed, using the name by which Nate was known by a goodly number of tribes. "Have you had any trouble with my people in the past few moons?"

The query surprised Nate. Ever since he had arranged a truce between the Shoshones and the Utes, who had been squabbling over a remote valley special to both peoples, the Utes had left him alone. They no longer made annual raids against him. "No. Why do you ask?"

"Some of the young hotheads think that you are to blame for the death of a warrior named Buffalo Hump and his family."

"I have not rubbed out a Ute since the truce."

Two Owls signed, "I believe you. But the younger ones do not know you like I do, Grizzly Killer. They still see all whites as our bitter enemies. Were it not for my influence, they would already have paid you a visit."

The knowledge made Nate wonder how long his family would be safe if anything were to happen to the chief. "Tell me of this Buffalo Hump."

"He was an old warrior, well past his prime. In his time he counted over twenty coup, and he was widely respected." Two Owls lowered his hands a moment, his sadness obvious. "Every Thunder Moon he liked to journey to Dream Lake, where he went on his first vision quest when he was only fourteen winters old. He would take his wife and two daughters with him."

Nate knew of Dream Lake, a small, pristine jewel fed by runoff, one of the highest lakes in the Rockies. It was located about 15 miles from his cabin.

"This last time Buffalo Hump did not return as expected and warriors were sent to learn why,"

Two Owls signed. His gestures became sharper as anger crept over him. "They found him and his family butchered. Things had been done to him that even we would not do to our enemies. His wife had also been mutilated. As for his daughters—" Two Owls stopped.

"There is no need to go on," Nate signed.

For a minute the chief simply sat there, glowering at the sky. At last he sighed. "It was a great loss, Grizzly Killer. Buffalo Hump and I were very close. I relied on his wisdom during councils."

"There were no clues to who did it?"

"One," Two Owls signed, staring Nate in the eyes. "The warriors found a strange knife. It is no longer than my longest finger and folds in half so that the blade fits into a groove in the wooden handle."

The revelation was deeply disturbing. Until that moment, Nate had suspected that other Indians were responsible for the old warrior's death since few whites ever ventured anywhere near Dream Lake. But based on the description, the knife found had to be a jackknife, and only whites carried them. Warriors preferred big-bladed butcher and hunting knives. Indian women liked smaller knives, but the blades needed to be rigid and thin for the sewing and hide work the women did.

"Those who trap beaver carry this kind of knife," Two Owls signed.

"I know."

"Since Wolverine and you live closest to Dream Lake, the two of you were blamed. I came to talk to both of you. We went to Wolverine's wooden lodge first but he was not there."

Wolverine was none other than Nate's mentor, Shakespeare McNair, who in his younger days had been a regular hellion in battle and thereby earned the name.

"I have not seen Wolverine in over a moon," Nate signed, suddenly worried that whoever slew Buffalo Hump might have done the same to Shakespeare and Shakespeare's Flathead wife, Blue Water Woman.

Two Owls pursed his lips. "You did my people a great service when you helped us settle matters with the Shoshones. I am in your debt, Grizzly Killer. But I do not know how long I can hold the young warriors back. Many of them thirst for vengeance. The only way to put out the fires in their hearts is to find the ones who are truly to blame. Since your kind are the culprits, you would have a better chance of doing so than I would."

The chief was being as polite as could be, but the underlying message could not have been more sinister had he made a declaration of war. Either Nate tracked down the real culprits or the Utes would come against him in greater numbers than ever before, and there was nothing Two Owls could do to prevent it. His family wouldn't stand a prayer.

"I am sorry, Grizzly Killer," Two Owls signed. "You have taught me that not all whites are bad medicine, but my people do not see you through my eyes."

"How much time do I have?"

"There is no way to tell. I will try to get word to you if an attack is planned."

Nate made the sign for gratitude, which was

done by extending both hands flat, palms down, and sweeping them in a curve outward and downward.

The war chief of the Utes grunted and rode off to rejoin his fellows. The quartet then trotted to the southwest. Nate stared until they were out of sight, his mind awhirl with the life-or-death situation his family faced. He wasn't about to move, no matter what. Yet how was he going to find the guilty parties when they were long gone, their tracks no doubt long since obliterated by the elements?

Hurrying over the hillock, Nate mounted the black stallion and applied his heels. He no longer cared how tired the packhorses might be. Winona, Zach, and Evelyn were more important.

Twilight veiled the majestic Rockies in a gray shroud when Nate paused on the lip of a ridge overlooking his valley. The sight of the familiar emerald lake brought a sense of relief. He was almost home.

Descending to the valley floor took over half an hour. He expected to see smoke curling from the stone chimney of their cabin, but when the log structure came into view, it appeared deserted. There was no smoke. The door was closed. The leather flaps to both windows were drawn.

A kernel of fear formed in Nate—fear that he was too late, that a band of young warriors had already struck. He fairly flew the last quarter of a mile and sprang from the saddle before the stallion came to a standstill.

Hawken in hand, Nate threw open the door and burst inside. The single large room was empty. No fire had been kindled in the fireplace. The supper dishes had not been placed on the table.

"Winona?" Nate called out. "Zach?"

Dashing back outside, Nate ran around to the corral he had built. It was as empty as the cabin. All the other horses were gone: Winona's mare, Zach's calico, and their extra pack animals.

There could only be one explanation, and it practically froze Nate's blood in his veins. A Ute band had struck, carted off his family, and stolen their stock.

Racing to the stallion, Nate vaulted into the saddle and made a hasty circuit of the cabin, seeking sign. Thanks to the expert teaching of Shakespeare and Shoshone friends such as Touch The Clouds and Drags The Rope, Nate could track as well as any man alive.

At the southwest corner of the corral Nate found where a lot of horses had made off briskly into the forest. The freshness of the tracks, indicated by clods of earth which had not yet had time to dry out, gave him hope. He figured the attack had taken place within the past hour. So the Utes couldn't have gotten all that far.

At a mad gallop Nate raced in pursuit. He left the packhorses standing near the cabin. They wouldn't stray off, not with plenty of grass and water handy.

By now the twilight had faded to the point where Nate could barely see the well-marked trail. He worried that darkness would force him to curtail his pursuit until morning. Thinking of his wife in the clutches of hostile warriors was almost enough to give him fits.

Suddenly Nate sped into a meadow. At the opposite end something moved in the shadows.

On looking closer, he beheld riders and seven or eight horses. Elated that he had come on the Utes so soon, he whipped the Hawken to his shoulder and charged, throwing prudence to the cool wind.

The nearest rider raised a rifle. Nate curled his finger around the Hawken's trigger and fixed a quick bead. He was about to apply enough pressure to discharge the black powder when the oncoming rider whooped in delight.

"Pa! Pa! It's great to have you back!"

Nate King snapped the Hawken down and broke out in a cold sweat. In his unreasoning fear and haste he had almost put a lead ball into his own flesh and blood.

The boy galloped to his father's side, so overjoyed that he cackled crazily and slapped his thigh. "Land sakes, Pa. It took you long enough. Ma was getting a mite worried. I told her you'd probably gone plumb to Canada. You've always wanted to visit the North Country."

Laughing, Nate reached out and affectionately rubbed the youngster's tousled dark locks. "You're pretty near right, but I had to go up, not north. This time of year it's hard to find elk at the lower elevations. I had to climb a mountain so high I could have spit on the moon from where I stood before I found the herd I was looking for."

"Shucks, Pa. There ain't no mountain that high. Don't try your tall tales on me. I'm getting too old to believe those preposterous stories of you."

"Preposterous?" Nate said, pretending to be flustered. "Where'd you learn a two-dollar word like that? Have you been hanging around that no-account McNair again?"

"Pa!" young Zachary said. "Don't let him hear you talk like that or he's liable to get his feelings hurt."

"Son," Nate said, "that old coon has a hide thicker than a bull buffalo's. He's happiest when he can be as feisty as a riled bantam rooster, and he's feistiest when I'm picking on him. Trust me. Insults slide off his back like water off a duck."

Just then Nate smelled a tangy minty scent and looked up. The aromatic fragrance was one he had inhaled countless times since marrying the loveliest maiden in the Shoshone nation. Eleven years later, he still felt that way.

Winona King's features were as smooth as the day she had taken Nate for her husband. She wore a finely crafted buckskin dress, which she had made herself. Her raven tresses had been braided so she could strap a cradleboard to her back. Her white teeth flashing, she bent to give her man a warm kiss on the cheek. "We have missed you, husband."

"So I gather," Nate said, pleased by her show of emotion. As a general rule, Indians seldom went in for such public displays. Matters of the heart were confined to behind lodge walls.

"Did you bring back as much meat as we need to tide us over until winter?" Winona asked in her perfectly precise English.

It was a source of pride to Nate that she had mastered his tongue much more thoroughly than he had mastered hers. She was exceptionally intelligent. Shakespeare liked to say that Nate had married her for her intellect instead of her beauty, it being McNair's belief that a man who wed a woman smart enough for two came out even in the long run.

"I've brought plenty of meat," he said, "but I've also brought word of a heap of trouble. We have to talk."

"First greet your daughter."

Nate moved the stallion forward a step so he could lean to the right. A small bundle of joy beamed at him from out of the cradleboard. She cooed when he pecked her cheek. "Goodness gracious, precious. How you keep growing. The next time I come back from a hunting trip, I expect you'll have a beau."

Winona had the missing pack animals on a long lead. She swung her mare beside her son's mount and together they headed across the meadow.

"What the blazes are you doing out here anyway?" Nate asked as he fell into step beside her. "Did the packhorses get out of the corral?"

"No," Winona said. "They had been cooped up so long they were restless. We brought them out to the meadow and let them graze and wander a while."

"We would have been back sooner, Pa, but for that darn painter," Zach said.

"What painter?" Nate asked, all interest. Recently he'd nearly lost his life tangling with a panther, or mountain lion as some of the mountaineers called the big cats, and he had no interest in doing so again.

Zach bobbed his chin at a slope to the south. "Up there yonder. A little before sunset it set to hollering and screeching and spooked two of the horses. I had to fetch them before we could head on home."

"We haven't heard it in a while," Winona said. "I imagine it has wandered elsewhere by now."

As if to prove her wrong, in the pines directly ahead of them, a caterwauling cry rife with menace rent the night.

Chapter Three

Men and women who are genuinely brave do not think of themselves in a time of crisis. It is an undeniable mark of true courage that, when danger strikes, the courageous are more concerned with the welfare of others.

So it was to Nate King's credit that, the instant he heard the feral challenge of the savage cat, he goaded the black stallion out in front of his wife and offspring so that he was in a better position to protect them should the painter attack.

And it was equally to young Zach's credit that he did the same. Ablaze with excitement, the boy hefted his heavy Hawken to his shoulder and cocked the hammer.

"Don't shoot unless you see the varmint," Nate said. "A man who shoots at shadows can wind up with an empty gun when he needs it the most."

The cry had issued from an inky stand of trees

where the undergrowth was especially dense. Nate glued his eyes to the tract, seeking a telltale tawny flash that would be all the forewarning he had of the beast's onslaught. High grass rustled, but whether from the wind or the passage of a large form, he couldn't tell.

Nate was not about to give the painter the chance to spring on them from ambush. Sometimes the best way to handle a contrary critter, he had learned, was to give the critter a taste of its own medicine. With that notion in mind, he urged the stallion into a trot, straight at the high grass. Whooping and yipping like a demented coyote, he flapped his arms and legs.

The panther was there, all right. A feline shape streaked from concealment, but instead of charging, it made off to the south in smooth bounds that covered 15 feet at a time. In the bat of an eye it was lost among the vegetation.

Nate reined up and elevated his rifle but he held his fire when he saw there was no need for it. He spotted the mountain lion for a fraction of a second as it crossed a clearing; then it was gone for good.

"Darn," Zach said. "I was hoping to have me a new painter hide."

"Just be grateful it didn't draw blood," Nate said. He waited for Winona to catch up and took the lead rope from her. "Now let's get home before that cat has a change of heart and comes back for its supper."

Once the horses were safely bedded down and the elk meat lay on a counter in the corner of the cabin, Nate could finally unwind. He took a seat at their table and propped his feet on top. "I dried the strips proper, but ran out of salt before I was done," he said for his wife's benefit.

Winona was examining the jerky closely. "None of it spoiled. We will eat the unsalted meat over the next few days." Opening a cupboard he had constructed from soft pine, she removed a parfleche and began stuffing the jerked meat inside. "You did well, husband."

"I have my days," Nate said.

"You mentioned something about trouble, Pa," Zach said. He was seated on the bed, tickling Evelyn with a jay feather.

"That I did," Nate said and launched into the full story of his encounter with the Ute leader and the information that had been imparted.

"It was kind of Two Owls to warn us," Winona said afterward. "You are supposed to go off trapping soon. We would have been alone when the Utes came for us."

Zach straightened up. "But what do we do now that we know? We can't hardly fight off forty or fifty warriors at a time."

"There is only one thing we can do," Winona said. "We must find the ones who slew Buffalo Hump before the Utes drive us off or wipe us out."

It shouldn't have surprised Nate that his wife made the suggestion. Bred from infancy to be worthy partners of their warrior husbands, Shoshone women could be as fierce as their mates when the need arose. He had seen firsthand how they fought like tigers when their villages were attacked. But he was unwilling to put her in danger when there was an alternative. "What's this we business? I aim to go after them by my lonesome."

"And what will we be doing?" Winona asked. "Are we supposed to stay here doing nothing?"

"No. I figured that the kids and you can stay with your uncle while I tend to whoever brought this aggravation down on our heads."

"I see," Winona said, clipping the two words as if spitting them out rather than speaking them. "You would feel better if we were safe in a Shoshone village."

"I'm glad you understand." Nate grinned, trying to appease her, although he knew full well he was in for a dose of her temper.

Winona gave him the sort of look that could melt ice at ten paces. "You want us to cower among our kin while you risk your life on our behalf?"

"Who said anything about cowering?" Nate asked. "I just think it's for the best, what with you having Zach and Evelyn to look out after and all."

"We have them to look after, husband." Winona walked to the table. "In the past, when they were younger, I was content to stay here while you went off time and time again. But no longer. This time I will not stay behind. Our whole family is in peril, so we will deal with the problem as a family."

"But what about the boy and Evelyn?"

"Zach is old enough to handle himself. Didn't he save you from those Gros Ventres a while ago? And who was it who escaped from the Blackfeet all on his own?"

"True, true," Nate said. "But this is different."

"Tell me how."

Nate opened his mouth to speak, but for the life of him he couldn't think of a convincing argument. Truth was, she had a valid point. In frontier terms, Zach was on the verge of manhood. Sheltering the youth would do him more harm than good in the long run. A body had to learn to stand on his own two feet at an early age or he never would.

Nate glanced at his son and saw the earnest appeal in the boy's eyes. Zach wanted to help, to prove he could carry his weight. It would be wrong to deny him.

Then there was Winona. Nate knew she had an independent streak in her a yard wide, and once she set her mind to something, only an act of the Almighty could change it.

In this case Nate couldn't blame her for wanting to lend a hand. She had every right. Her family and home were at risk. What sort of husband would he be if he raised a fuss over her doing what came naturally?

"Well?" Winona said.

Sitting up, Nate regarded his wife and son soberly. "I must be as crazy as a loon. But I'm not about to try to buck you on this. The danger is to our whole family, so as a family we'll clear ourselves of blame."

Zach came off the bed as if shot from a cannon and leaped so high into the air his head nearly brushed the ceiling. Like a virile young wolf reveling in being alive, he howled and spun. "Thank you, Pa! I'll pull my own weight. You'll see. Whatever you want, whatever you say—"

"Calm down, son, before you bust a gut," Nate

said grinning. "I know you'll do right fine." His grin evaporated as he pondered how best to proceed. Their first step was to find those responsible for the grisly deaths. But how, when they lacked a single shred of information that might identify the guilty party or parties other than the jackknife? "Maybe we'll have to make a trip to Dream Lake."

"What could we hope to find after all this time?" Winona said. "It has been over a month."

"I'm open to a better idea," Nate said.

Zach was listening intently. Now that he had been given a chance to show his folks that he was no longer the small boy they all too often treated him as, he was bound and determined not to let them down. "I have an idea," he said tentatively.

"What is it?" Nate asked.

"Well, Two Owls thinks whites are to blame. If there have been any strangers in this neck of the woods in the past month or so, doesn't it stand to reason, Pa, that some of the other mountain men have seen them?"

The insight was so obvious that Nate was amazed he hadn't thought of it himself. There were at least two trappers he knew of who lived within a few day's ride of Dream Lake. Paying them a visit might prove rewarding. "I think you've got the right idea, son. We'll head for Old Bill's place at first light."

"Bill Zeigler's?" Winona said sharply.

Nate nodded. "He lives closest to Dream Lake."

"But is it safe? You know the horrible stories told about him. What if they are true?"

"It's a risk we'll have to take."

* * *

Miles from the King cabin, six men sat around a crackling fire. Several held tin cups filled with black coffee. One chewed loudly on jerked buffalo meat. A string of tired horses had been tethered nearby.

Earl Lassiter sank to one knee to refill his cup. He cursed when he accidentally rubbed the back of his hand on the scalding pot and pain lanced up his arm. One of the others snickered but fell abruptly silent when Lassiter glared at him. "Do you think it's funny that I burned myself, Yost?"

The stringbean addressed shook his scarecrow head vigorously. "No, sir, Earl. Not on your life. I just sort of thought the look on our face was a little bit comical, is all."

"Oh?" Lassiter's voice was as cold as ice, as hard as granite. "Maybe I should shove the pot down your britches and see how comical you act."

Yost gulped. Every member of the gang knew it wasn't very smart to rile their leader. There was no telling when he might unexpectedly snap and fly into a fit of violence that made grizzlies seem tame by comparison. "I didn't mean anything. Honest. You've no call to be so testy."

"I don't like being laughed at," Lassiter growled.

He never had. As a boy, he'd been notorious for pounding anyone who had the gall to poke fun at him. To his way of thinking, to be mocked was the ultimate insult. It reminded Earl of all those awful childhood years when his drunkard father had belittled him every time he turned around. He'd been jeered, slapped silly, and called all kinds of names: jackass, idiot, good for nothing, plumb worthless, and many, many more. The memory was enough to make Lassiter clench his fists in budding rage.

One of the others noticed. He was much older than his rough companions, his hair the hue of freshly fallen snow. Ben Kingslow was his name, and he took it on himself to avert possible bloodshed by clearing his throat and saying, "I swear! That squaw sure did put up a scrap, didn't she? It's too bad we couldn't have kept her alive and brought her with us."

"Why?" asked a stocky man partial to a blue cap. "So she could slit our throats in our sleep the first chance she got? No thank you. I'm glad that Earl had Bear put a ball into her."

The giant with the greasy hair and clothes chuckled. "Did you see the way she squirmed after she was shot, Dixon? I saw a snake do that once after its head had been chopped off."

Ben Kingslow was studying Lassiter on the sly. "I just meant it would be nice to have a woman or two to accommodate those of us who might be inclined at night. None of us have been getting it regularly since we left the States."

Dixon chuckled. "I didn't know old goats your age could still get a rise."

"My age?" Kingslow snorted. "Haven't you heard, you young pup, that the older the wine, the better it is? I'll have you know that, the last time I was with a woman, she compared me to a tree."

A scrawny man whose lower lip had been split long ago in a knife fight spoke up for the first time. "A dead tree, I'll bet."

At this there was rowdy laughter.

"That's putting the geezer in his place, Snip," Dixon said. "To hear him talk, you'd think he had females fawning over him everywhere he goes."

Kingslow was pleased to note a smile curl Lassiter's lips. For the time being trouble had been averted. But sooner or later someone would say the wrong thing and he wouldn't be there to bail whoever it was out.

Only one soul there did not join in the mirth. The half-breed sat apart, his arms folded across his chest, his rifle in his lap. "I do not care about women," he said gravely in his heavily accented English. "I want my share of the gold."

Bear thumped his thigh in irritation. "So did I, Cano. It got my dander up when we couldn't find that bastard's cache."

"Don't fret yourself," Lassiter said. "There are a lot more sheep out here waiting to be fleeced. One of these times we'll strike it rich so we can all go back to civilization and live like kings."

"That would be fine by me," Dixon said, "but I doubt all the mountain men combined have that much money."

"They have proved slim pickings," Lassiter said, "leaner than I counted on. So maybe it's time we did like all good hunters do when the game they're after proves scarce."

"Which is?" Bear asked.

"Go after different game," Lassiter said, leaning back and propping an elbow under him. "I've heard tell that a lot of pilgrims have taken to heading for the Oregon Country by way of South Pass and the Green River Valley region."

Snip poked a stick into the flames. "What makes you think we'll be any better off?"

"Think for a minute," Lassiter said. "Most of these pilgrims travel in big old wagons piled high with all their worldly goods. Odds are they also tote all their money along, since it's not likely they'd leave their nest eggs behind."

Greed sparkled in Dixon's eyes. "I'll bet you that some of those goods are worth a lot, besides. Why, we could have full pokes in no time."

Lassiter took a long sip of coffee. "My notion exactly, hos. So what say we drift up toward the Green River and keep our eyes skinned for plump wagons ripe for the plucking?"

"This is your best idea yet." Kingslow saw fit to compliment the plan to make up for his blunder earlier. "We'll be hip deep in bootie."

Dixon twisted and scanned the surrounding forest. "What about the Blood, Earl? Think he'll go along with the scheme?"

"Brule has stuck with us this far," Lassiter said. "I doubt he has anywhere else to go."

Scrawny Snip gave a little shudder. "I don't mind admitting that he gives this coon a bad case of the fidgets every time he looks at me. I don't rightly see why we keep him around when he might up and scalp the bunch of us one night while we're sleeping. It's no damn secret that his kind hate our kind worse than anything else."

"Usually that's the case," Lassiter said. "But you have to remember that Brule hates his own people just as much because they booted him out of the tribe. It was a lucky day for me when I stumbled on him up by the Tetons."

Ben Kingslow had heard of that fateful meeting several times since throwing in with Lassiter's wild bunch. Lassiter had been trapping during the spring season when he'd come on the Blood at the top of a precipice.

The warrior had been on the verge of throwing himself off. Apparently Brule had been so shamed at being made an outcast, he hadn't cared whether he lived or died.

"We need the buck," Lassiter said, bringing Kingslow back to the present. "He's a better tracker than any of us will ever be. And he has an uncanny knack for sniffing out trouble."

"It's like having a caged panther," Snip said. "You never know when it might turn on you."

Dixon appeared afflicted by the same unease. "Where is he anyway? Why does he always go off by himself at night? Ain't our company good enough for him?"

"He's a loner at heart," Lassiter said. "But he's always by our side when we need him the most, so I don't want any of you saying anything to him. If you have a grievance, you go through me."

"Think I'm loco?" Dixon said. "I'm not about to get into a racket with that red devil. He's the meanest son of a bitch alive. You can tell just by looking into his eyes."

Earl Lassiter set down his empty cup. "Maybe he is. So what? Think of the bright side."

"What bright side?"

"If anyone comes after us, I'll just sic Brule on him. As much as that Blood enjoys shedding blood, no one will last two minutes."

Bold strokes of pink and yellow framed the pale eastern horizon when Nate King stepped from his warm cabin into the chill morning air and around to the rough-hewn corral. Hardly half an hour was required to saddle the three mounts and load provisions onto three packhorses. When he led the animals around front, he found his loved ones waiting for him. Winona and the baby were bundled in a heavy green shawl he had traded for at a prior rendezvous.

There were no locks to make secure, no bolts to be thrown. The door was simply closed, the windows covered.

This was the high country, where thievery was rare. Anyone caught stealing was likely to be shot on sight, which served to discourage those inclined to step over the line.

In New York City it had been different. How well Nate remembered the growing epidemic of robbery and assaults that had made life there so miserable. Footpads had roamed at will, secure in the knowledge that if they were apprehended they would likely get off with a slap on the wrist or a small fine.

Nate never tired of thinking about the startling contrasts between life in the States and life in the wilderness. In New York the people were crammed together like rats in a run-down tenement. Small wonder they snapped at one another all the time and couldn't get along except during emergencies, when their common humanity forged a temporary bond.

In the Rockies, men and women were truly free. They behaved as they pleased, doing what they wanted when they wanted. There was no overcrowding. There were no power-hungry politicians dictating how folks should live. None of the pressures New Yorkers experienced every single day of their sad lives existed.

Consequently, Nate had never met a happier lot of people than the mountaineers and Indians who inhabited the mountains. As a rule, if one excluded the hostile tribes, they were friendlier than their counterparts back east. They were more trusting. Best of all, they respected one another. There was none of that casual contempt Easterners unconsciously cultivated.

Nate would never go back to live in the States. He had ventured to the frontier for all the wrong reasons and discovered the right reasons to stay. Personal freedom, individual happiness, robust health—they all mattered more than the few conveniences civilization had to offer.

Such was Nate King's train of thought as he led his family northward out of their precious valley. Once on the ridge, he bore to the northwest.

From the lofty rampart, they watched the golden sun rise into the azure sky. Nate always found dawn to be invigorating. The rosy splendor, with its promise of life renewed for another day, caused him to regard the world in which he lived with abiding respect and reverence.

From the ridge Nate descended into a verdant valley where a small herd of shaggy mountain buffalo grazed. Deer moved among the trees. Ravens soared with outstretched wings on uplifting air currents.

Nate reveled in the grandeur. He took a deep breath, and heard a horse trot up next to his.

"Pa, I wanted to thank you for bringing me along," Zachary said. "It means a lot to me."

"So I gathered," Nate said. "I suppose I'd better

get used to having you do more and more as you get older. It's hard though, son. I can't stand the idea of you coming to harm, so I try to protect you more than I should."

"Do all fathers feel the same way?"

"Most do, I expect," Nate said. "My pa was the kind who never let me do anything for myself. I always had to do things his way, whether I liked it or not. Why, I was ten before he'd let me go to the store alone."

"You're joshing."

"I wish I was," Nate said. He pulled his beaver hat lower so the wind wouldn't snatch it off at an inopportune moment.

"I've been meaning to ask you," Zach said. "Last night ma acted upset when you mentioned going to visit this Zeigler feller. Doesn't she like him?"

"She's never met the man."

"Then why was she so bothered?

"There are some who say Old Bill isn't quite right in the head."

"How so?"

Nate looked at his son. "Some folks claim he's a cannibal."

Chapter Four

Zachary King had heard of cannibals, of course, but he had never in his wildest imaginings suspected he would actually meet one.

Tall tales were a staple of the mountain men; swapping yarns around a campfire was a favorite entertainment. Most of them had to do with living in the wild. Trappers told of vicious beasts they had slain, of narrow escapes from hostiles, of which streams were best for catching beaver and which were trapped out.

Now and then, however, the talk had nothing to do with the mountains. Men spoke of the places they hailed from, the varied sights they had witnessed in their travels. Several of the trappers had been seafaring men before they took to raising beaver for a living, and their exotic and thrilling accounts were some of Zach's favorites.

One night in particular Zach had never forgotten. It had been at the rendezvous, four years earlier. A lumbering slab of a man by the name of Gristle Jack had riveted the boy with chilling stories of outlandish peoples in other lands.

"Let me tell you about Africa," Gristle Jack had said, his eyes alight with the reflection of dancing flames. "I was there once, you see. On board a slaver. And the things I saw and learned, you wouldn't believe."

"Tell us," a trapper said.

"Well, why do you think everyone calls Africa the Dark Continent?" Gristle Jack said. "It's the natives. There are as many black men in Africa as there are whites in this country. More, I'd say. And they're as different in their ways as we are in ours. Some are as civilized as we are. They're the ones who sell slaves to plantation owners in the South. Others run around half naked and carry spears and clubs. They're the ones a man has to watch out for."

"How so?" someone had asked.

"Why, some of the tribes are cannibals. They like to plunk their captives in huge pots and boil the poor souls until the flesh is nicely cooked. Then they all sit down to a fine feast, chewing away with their pointed teeth."

"Pointed teeth?" a scoffer said.

"As the Lord is my witness," Gristle Jack said. "I heard that they file their teeth to make them as sharp as daggers. And some of them stick bones through their ears or else through their nose. I swear! I saw them with my own eyes!"

Now, four days after leaving the cabin, Zach gazed anxiously down on the narrow, shadowy valley where Bill Zeigler lived and felt a shudder go through him. He pictured Old Bill with filed, tapered teeth and bones in his pierced ears and nose, and he wondered if the old man had a huge pot in which to cook his victims.

"Are you all right, son?" Nate asked.

Zach glanced around and self-consciously cleared his throat. He was embarrassed that his father had seen the worry on his face and tried to explain it away by saying, "I was just thinking that maybe we should go down there alone, Pa. It might not be safe for ma and sis."

Winona overheard. "I was taking care of myself long before you were born. If Old Bill is not careful, you will see how capable I am."

It was a continual source of amusement and irritation to Winona that the males in her family treated her as if she were a fragile flower that would fall to pieces at the slightest touch. Shoshone warriors never regarded women so.

Having mulled over the matter at length, Winona had reached the conclusion that Nate did not think of her as inferior in any way. Time and again he had admitted that she was a fine shot, a skilled rider, and a competent provider.

No, her husband's attitude stemmed from his upbringing. Winona had questioned him and learned most white men shared his view. At an early age the idea was instilled in them that women were in need of constant protection. It was ridiculous.

Winona knew that her husband tried to see her more as a Shoshone warrior would, but it was hard to break habits so old, so ingrained. Unfortunately, at times Zach seemed to be afflicted with the same attitude. She could only hope that one day they both came to their senses.

A few yards in front of her, Nate stood in the stirrups to survey the valley closely. He had never been there before, but he had been told how to reach it by a trapper who had. Mountain men routinely swapped information having to do with routes of travel, the locations of streams and lakes, and more.

Bill Zeigler had chosen a forbidding spot in a remote chain of stark peaks. If it was privacy he craved, he had found it. There was no more isolated valley in all the Rockies.

Thanks to the high summits ringing Zeigler's sanctuary, it lay in shadow most of the day. A game trail meandered to the valley floor through densely packed pines standing like silent sentinels along the pathway.

Nate assumed the lead, the Hawken propped on his thigh. According to an acquaintance of his, Frenchy Smith, Zeigler lived in a dirt dugout on a knoll overlooking a deep stream. Nate was on edge. He didn't like taking his family down there but he would be wasting his breath if he tried to persuade them to stay on the slope.

As Nate rode, he recollected the story told about Old Bill. Ten or 12 years earlier—no one could remember exactly when—Bill and his partner, Yerby, had gone off after beaver and been trapped in the high country by the first heavy snow. They had ended up being snowbound all winter. Came the spring, and only Bill made his way down to the rendezvous. Many asked about Yerby and were told that he had died in an avalanche.

Somehow, whispers got started. Loose lips

speculated that maybe Yerby had died differently, that maybe the sole reason Old Bill had survived was too ghastly to be believed.

Nate had never taken the tale seriously. Old Bill wasn't the first to be branded a cannibal. Every so often it would happen, and in nearly every instance, the rumors turned out to be nothing more than the gory handiwork of mountaineers with too much free time on their hands and too much alcohol in their systems.

Still, Nate felt uneasy. He wasn't a friend of Zeigler's, and Old Bill was known to be touchy about people dropping in on him out of the blue. Zeigler might be inclined to shoot first and learn who they were later.

The pines were eerily quiet. The wind whispered through the jade-green needles, but the birds and beasts who dwelt in the forest were as quiet as the great slabs of rock on the heights above.

Halfway down, Nate spied the stream, flanking a mountain to the north. To reach it, he had to cross a lot of open ground. They would be exposed, vulnerable.

So intent was Nate on the grassy flatland, he almost missed hearing the faint tread of a human foot to his right. Almost, but not quite. Twisting, he saw a buckskin-garbed figure hurtle at him from out of the brush. He tried to bring the Hawken to bear but the figure had already leaped atop a small boulder and from there sprang straight at him. He heard Zach's cry of warning even as his attacker slammed into him. The rifle went flying when he was bowled from the saddle.

Nate shoved free of the man's clutching grasp

as he fell. He hit on his right shoulder and rolled into a crouch, his left hand stabbing for a pistol. His assailant pounced before he could draw and they both went down. A knife glittered above him.

Thrusting his arms out, Nate sought to prevent the blade from sinking into his flesh. He finally saw the craggy, grizzled face of Old Bill Zeigler poised against the backdrop of foliage, his features aglow with bloodlust, his eyes gleaming with demonical intensity. For a harrowing moment Nate thought that the tales must be true, and he braced himself as the older man's arm tensed to arc downward.

Then there was the drum of flying hooves and from out of nowhere swept the smooth stock of a rifle. It caught Zeigler on the side of the head and toppled him into the weeds.

In a flash Nate was on his feet, a flintlock filling each brawny hand. A few feet away stood Zach's calico, the boy holding the Hawken he had used to brain old Zeigler.

"I'm obliged, son," Nate said.

Zach swelled with pride. He had acted without thinking, doing the first thing that came to mind. His mother, he noticed, was gazing fondly at him in that way she often did when she was enormously pleased by something he had done.

When a low groan emanated from the weeds, Nate strode over to the shabby pair of patched moccasins jutting into the open and whacked one with a foot. "Get up and explain yourself."

The groan was repeated, louder and longer. Old Bill Zeigler slowly sat up, both hands pressed to his head, his eyes squeezed tight shut. "Oh,

Lordy. My achin' noggin. What the devil happened? Did a tree fall on me?"

"You tried to kill me, damn you," Nate said.

Zeigler lowered his arms, revealing a nasty knot where the stock had slammed into him. He cocked his head and squinted at the four of them, focusing on Nate. "I know you. Met you at the rendezvous, as I recollect. King, ain't it?"

"Nate King."

"This must be your family," Old Bill said pleasantly. Shaking his head as if to clear cobwebs, he pushed upright. His knees nearly buckled and he swayed a few seconds, then cackled and slapped his thigh. "Which one of you walloped the daylights out of me?"

"I did, sir," Zach said nervously. He felt a little guilty having hurt the man until he reminded himself that his pa's life had been at stake.

"You're a dandy walloper, lad," Old Bill said without a trace of malice. "You must go around whippin' the tar out of grizzlies in your spare time."

Zachary laughed, pleased there were no hard feelings. "No, sir. My pa is the one they call Grizzly Killer. He's rubbed out more than any man alive, white or Indian."

Old Bill shifted his attention back to Nate. "That's right. Kilt about a hundred, I heard tell."

"Hardly," Nate said dryly. The old-timer had dropped the knife and wasn't armed with pistols or a tomahawk, so Nate felt safe in wedging his flintlocks under his wide leather belt. "Now suppose you tell us why you tried to bury that pigsticker in me."

The grizzled mountain man looked down at the ground and shuffled his feet from side to side as if embarrassed. "I'm plumb sorry about that, King. To tell the truth, I mistook you for hostiles."

"In broad daylight?" Nate said skeptically. "I'll admit that a greenhorn might mistake me for an Indian, but a seasoned mountaineer like you should be able to tell the difference."

"Should be," Old Bill said, frowning. "I don't rightly know if I should let the cat out of the bag, but I guess it can't do no harm."

"What are you talking about?"

"My peepers." Bill raised a finger to his eyes. "They're not what they used to be. Why, once I could see a sparrow on the wing half a mile away. Nowadays I'm lucky if I can make out a darned elk at twenty feet." He mentioned at the trail. "When I first spotted you folks, you were all a blur. I figured you must be some of those pesky Utes who have aggravated me something fierce over the years." Bill paused. "I'm just glad I didn't have my rifle. I'm not the shot I once was, but I might have hit one of you anyway."

The mention of a rifle set Nate to searching for his Hawken. He found it lying a few feet away. "I'm sorry to hear about your problem," he said. A man needed all his senses intact to survive in the wild. "If you're that bad off, maybe you should give some thought to moving down out of the mountains."

"And do what? Live at one of the forts? I'd go crazy being cooped up all the time. And I'm sure as blazes not going back to the States. I'm not about to spend the rest of my days sitting on some street corner, begging for pennies. I may not have much, but I've got my dignity."

Nate saw the knife lying seven feet away and retrieved it for the man. "Here."

"Thanks." Old Bill wiped the blade on his leggings, then shoved it into a sheath that had seen better days years ago. His buckskins were also in dire need of mending. "Listen. What say I make it up to you by having you folks for a meal? I managed to bring down a buck yesterday so there's plenty of fresh meat. It's early yet, I know, but I don't often get company. And the older I get, the less I object to having people stop by."

"We'd be grateful," Nate said, although he would have preferred to ask a few questions and be on his way. There was a touch of melancholy about the older man that tugged at his heartstrings. He looked at Winona for confirmation and she nodded.

"I'm the one who's grateful." Old Bill brightened. "I haven't had a soul to talk to in weeks."

Nate opened his mouth to glean more details but the old mountain man moved off down the trail as quickly as a jackrabbit.

"Come on! Don't dawdle! I'll scoot on ahead and have the coffee on before you get there. Just follow the stream west a ways. You can't miss my place."

"There's no need—" Nate said and stopped. Bill was moving with remarkable speed for someone who couldn't see very well. In moments he rounded a bend and was gone.

Zach chuckled. "He sure is excited about having us to vittles. Do you reckon he's awful lonely, Pa?"

It was Winona who responded. "He must be. Men and women are not meant to spend their days alone. That is why my people prefer village life to going off by ourselves, as your father's people do." She clucked her mare into motion. "There are many things about whites I do not understand, husband, but liking to live alone has always puzzled me the most."

"Do tell," Nate said while mounting. In all the years they had been together, she had never once mentioned it to him. "Maybe it has something to do with having different natures, sort of like buffalo and bears. Buffalo like to live together in great herds, bears like to live alone in dens."

"Which is the right way for folks to be?" Zach asked.

Nate urged the stallion and packhorse into following them. "It's not etched in stone, son. It all depends on the person. You have to do what is right for you and not care what anyone else thinks."

"I don't think I'd ever like to live all by myself," Zach said. "I'd need a family, at least, just like you, Pa."

They fell silent until they reached the gurgling stream, which ran surprisingly deep and swift. A clearly defined trail pointed the way to the knoll, hundreds of yards off. Situated at the tree line, it blended into the wall of vegetation as if part of it. A casual observer would never suspect that someone lived there.

Bill Zeigler was as good as his word. On reining up in front of the dugout, Nate smelled smoke and saw a thin tendril wafting from a small hole atop the knoll. As he tethered the horses, part of the slope swung outward and there stood Zeigler, framed in a doorway.

"Howdy again, folks!"

Zach gawked in astonishment at the cleverly concealed door. "I declare! I've never seen the like in all my born days!"

"An old cuss like you?" Zeigler said. He gave the planks a whack. "Came up with this idea all by myself. I had a heck of a time gettin' Wyeth to bring me some metal hinges from St. Louis. He claimed I was the only trapper in the Rockies who had ever ordered hinges, and there wouldn't be any profit in it since he only had to bring three."

"That sounds like Wyeth," Nate said, referring to the trader who had once supplied provisions at the rendezvous and later built Fort Hall. "That man won't do anything unless there's a profit in it."

Old Bill propped the door open with a stick he kept handy for the purpose and beckoned. "Come on in, folks. Make yourself to home and we'll chaw a while." He stepped aside to permit them to enter, then did a double take on seeing the cradleboard. "A sprout! Land sakes! I didn't know you was totin' a young'un, ma'am."

"Evelyn is her name. I'm Winona."

Zeigler was taken aback when she offered her hand. He took it gingerly, as if afraid he'd break it if he squeezed too hard. "It's a pleasure to make your acquaintance. I can see your husband is a man who likes women of quality."

Winona stepped inside and promptly wished she hadn't. A rank odor assailed her nostrils, and the interior was as filthy as it was possible to be and still be habitable. Piles of hides, some half rotten because they had not been cured properly, lined both walls. A bundle of blankets and robes at the far end served as the bed. In the center sat a small table and two stools, a stove, and a bench littered with tools and traps.

"Don't mind the mess," Old Bill said. "Every two or three years I give the place a thorough cleaning. I reckon it's about due."

"So it would seem," Winona said politely.

"Sit anywhere you like," Old Bill said. "I'm not fussy at all."

Winona did not see how any human being could live under such conditions. She picked her way with care to a stool and took a seat after removing the cradleboard so she could hold Evelyn in her lap.

The stench hardly bothered Zach. He had smelled much worse, like that time after the Shoshones conducted a buffalo surround and the prairie had been choked with carcasses being roasted by the scorching sun. The horrible stink and the swarming flies had about gagged him.

Nate, however, covered his mouth with a hand and pretended to cough. Breathing shallow, he took the stool next to his wife and leaned the Hawken against the table.

"This is wonderful, just wonderful," Old Bill said as he puttered about hanging an unlit lantern on a peg, moving some hides closer to the side of the dugout, and collecting battered cups for their coffee. "I sure am glad you folks stopped on by."

"We had a reason," Nate said. "We're trying to

find out who killed an old Ute by the name of Buffalo Hump."

In the act of setting the cups on the table, Old Bill paused. "A Ute, you say? What does it matter who killed him? They're all a bunch of murderin' skunks in my book."

"Not all of them," Nate said and detailed the reason for their visit. "You can appreciate the fix we're in. We have to find the guilty parties or risk losing everything that means anything to us."

Zeigler had listened with rising interest. "I'd like to help you, King. But the fact is that not a single stranger has paid me a visit in pretty near a year. The last man who did stop by was Jeremiah Sawyer, just about four weeks ago. He lives northwest of here in Crow country. About a two-day ride, is all. Maybe he can help you."

"I know Jeremiah," Nate said, not showing his disappointment that the visit to Old Bill hadn't panned out. Going to see Sawyer might prove equally as useless but it was better than doing nothing. "We'll head for his lodge at dawn."

"I'll be glad to guide you there," Zeigler said.

"That's all right. We'll manage."

"It'll be hard if you've never been there. His place is as out of the way as mine is. I can shave half a day off the trip if you're willing to push yourselves."

The prospect was appealing. "Let me talk it over with my wife," Nate said. Clasping her elbow, he escorted Winona from the cramped dugout. The cool evening air was downright intoxicating. He inhaled the sweet pine scent with relish.

"Thank you, husband," Winona said softly. "I did not know how much longer I could stand it in there. If a member of my tribe were to keep his lodge in the same condition Old Bill keeps his dugout, the man would be shunned by everyone."

"Should we refuse his help?" Nate asked.

Winona pondered before answering. She was glad that her husband often relied on her judgment when making decisions of importance to both of them. It wasn't a trait shared by all trappers. From other Shoshone women who had become the wives of whites, she had learned that by and large the trappers did as they pleased without regard for the feelings of the women. Several Shoshones had even been beaten for questioning their husband's actions.

"If he can save us half a day," Winona said, "we should accept his offer. It worries me, being gone from our cabin for so long. Should the Utes come while we are gone, they might burn it down to spite us."

"I was thinking the same thing," Nate said. He was also questioning how the old mountain man would be able to lead them when it would be difficult for Zeigler to keep track of landmarks. "You stay out here while I go have a few more words with him." He walked past Zach, who stood by the entrance.

Winona turned and admired the blazed of color painting the sky. She observed her son move toward the horses, then stare eastward and freeze. Whirling, she learned why, and gooseflesh erupted all over her body.

Lumbering across the stream toward the dugout was a huge grizzly.

Chapter Five

Nate King hardly got a word out of his mouth when his son bawled his name and a tremendous roar smote his ears. He was outside in a half-dozen bounds, the short hairs of his neck prickling when he beheld a veritable monster of a grizzly upright on its hind legs.

It had been many months since last Nate had tangled with a grizzly. When he first arrived in the mountains, it seemed as if every time he turned around he ran into one of the savage behemoths. More by circumstance than design he had survived time and again. But each harrowing nightmare had left him that much more anxious about future encounters.

So when Nate saw the enormous creature drop to all fours and move closer, it took him five seconds to bring his Hawken up to shoot. He knew that a single shot seldom dropped a griz.

More than likely he would only enrage the beast. But he couldn't stand there and do nothing. He had to act before his wife and children were torn to shreds.

Nate aimed at the grizzly's chest. Provided fate smiled on him, he might succeed in putting a ball into its lungs or heart.

"No! Don't shoot!"

Bill Zeigler raced from the dugout, flapping both arms like an ungainly demented bird trying to get off the ground. He leaped in front of the Hawken, blocking the shot with his body.

"Are you crazy?" Nate yelled. "Get out of the way before it's too late!"

"It's just Ulysses!" Old Bill cried. "He won't hurt any of us if we give him what he wants." So saying, the mountain man ran toward the bear.

Too flabbergasted to do anything except gape, Nate realized that Zeigler held a deer haunch. The grizzly had stopped and lifted its ponderous head to sniff the air, sounding for all the world like a bellows.

"Here, Ulysses!" Old Bill said, halting a dozen feet from the monster. "Just like always." Using both hands, he flung the haunch with all his might. It sailed end over end to plop down directly in front of the grizzly.

The bear sniffed at the meat a bit, then widened its maw and clamped down so hard the bone crunched. Its prize firmly held between its iron jaws, the lord of the Rockies ambled off across the stream and into the lush undergrowth beyond.

Nate liked to think that he had seen practically everything that had to do with the mountains and those who lived there. But never had he beheld the like of a man feeding a griz as if it were a prized pet instead of a living engine of destruction. Old Bill had to be missing a few marbles to pull such a stunt. Nate lowered the Hawken, shaking his head sadly when the old trapper waved at the departing bear.

"Thanks for not firing, King," Zeigler said. "That griz has been a friend of mine since before that boy of yours was born."

"You're playing with fire if you let that thing come around here whenever it pleases," Nate said. "Mark my words. It'll turn on you one of these days. Grizzlies are too unpredictable."

Old Bill clucked at him like a hen at an uppity chick. "Most griz are, I'll agree. But I came on that one when it was just a cub, shortly after it's ma was wiped out in a rock slide." He smiled at the memory. "I was going to blow its brains out when the thing started bawling like a baby. Then damned if it didn't waddle up to me and lick my hand. How could I shoot it after that?

"I fed it for weeks and weeks. Got to the point where the critter followed me around everywhere I went. Made trapping real hard, what with the beaver not about to go anywhere near a trap if there's griz scent in the area. Finally I had to shoo it off. But it still comes by every now and then, so I give it some grub like in the old days. It always goes on about its business without trying to hurt me."

Winona had clutched Evelyn to her bosom when the bear appeared, but now she cradled the child and said, "My people believe that only someone who possesses powerful medicine can call the great bear a brother. We will be honored to have you go with us tomorrow."

A peculiar grin twisted Old Bill's mouth. "Thank you, ma'am. You have no idea how much it means to me." He snickered for no apparent reason. "No idea at all."

His name, as best the whites could pronounce it, was Brule. He was a Blood warrior, a former member of one of the three tribes that made up the widely dreaded Blackfoot Confederacy.

He stood on a flat rock on a shelf of high land overlooking the next valley the men who followed him must cross, and he bowed his head in shame—shame that tormented him every time he thought about his former life, shame that he would never let those behind him see.

Brule was an outcast. He had done that which no warrior was ever allowed to do, committed the most heinous of acts. He had killed one of his own people.

It had been justified, in Brule's eyes. Minoka had tried to woo the maiden Brule had craved as his own. And when Brule had confronted him, Minoka had been rash enough to strike Brule across the face with an open palm.

No man could endure such an insult and still lay claim to manhood. Brule had done what any warrior would do. He had stabbed his rival through the heart.

Perhaps if it had been anyone but Minoka, Brule would still be among the Bloods. But Minoka's father was a war chief, a man of vast influence. That influence had been used to persuade the people of the village to cast Brule out, to expel him into the wilderness, where he was destined to roam until he died.

And he had roamed, for a while, until the aching loneliness had driven him to despair and he had resolved to end his existence by throwing himself off a cliff overlooking a lake in the Tetons.

Who could have foreseen that the white-eye named Lassiter would spot him and come to investigate? Lassiter had drawn a pistol and pointed it at him, but Brule had made no move to defend himself. He hadn't cared how his life ended, so long as it did.

Then the white man had asked him questions in sign language, and after Brule answered, Lassiter had put the pistol away and asked Brule to ride with him, to share in the killing and the plunder to come. For Lassiter had a great scheme to make himself rich among his kind, and in order to achieve his goal he needed to gather around him those of like minds.

Brule had not held any desire to be rich as the whites conceived of wealth. But he was a warrior born, and he did like the idea of going on the warpath against everyone and anyone—even his own people. For the more Brule thought about the injustice done him, the more he learned to despise those who had seen fit to cast him aside. Yet he could not shake the sense of shame.

Behind Brule a horse snorted. He turned and saw the breed, Cano, trailed by Lassiter and the rest of the whites. He bore no friendship for any of them. The breed, he tolerated. Lassiter, he owed a debt. The rest, he would as soon slit their throats as look at them.

Brule despised whites. His tribe, along with the

Blackfeet and the Piegans, exterminated any and all white men found in their territory.

He knew that the mountain men considered his people, and their allies, as little better than bloodthirsty animals who slaughtered for the sheer thrill of bloodletting.

Nothing could have been further from the truth, in Brule's opinion. While it was true the Bloods had always been a warlike people, they adhered to an honorable system of counting coup little different from other tribes. They were no more cruel or savage than the Sioux, the Cheyenne, or the Arapaho.

But in one major respect the Bloods did differ. They were heartily unwilling to stand idly by while their lands were overrun by the white vermin from the East.

It was a proven fact that the whites killed off wildlife at an unbelievable rate. In just a span of ten winters the trappers had severely reduced the number of beaver and mountain buffalo and were now slaying plains buffalo with an abandon the Bloods found appalling.

Brule's tribe regarded the whites as invaders who would eventually drive the Bloods from their homeland unless they were stopped before they became too numerous to resist.

For Brule to associate with whites, as he was doing now, required a measure of self-control he had rarely exercised. He couldn't stand to be near Lassiter and the others for more than a short while without feeling an urge to smash their heads in. They were filthy, arrogant, revolting. They looked down their superior noses at Brule and his kind, when in truth they were no better.

Brule had yet to make up his mind how long he would stay with them. He did know that before he left, he might slay every last one. For the time being, however, he was content to act as their scout and to share in any booty that interested him.

Already Brule had benefited. He had a new knife riding on his left hip and a steel tomahawk on his left. He carried a fine rifle instead of the cheap fusil he had formerly used. A large ammo pouch and a powder horn adorned his chest. He was better armed than ever before, which pleased him immensely.

Now, facing the others, Brule adopted a stony expression and squared his bronzed shoulder.

The half-breed addressed him in sign language. "Why have you stopped, my friend?" Cano asked.

Brule let the insult pass. He would never be friends to any bastard offspring of a white pig and a Dakota slut. But it served his purposed to pretend. Pivoting, he pointed at a column of smoke rising to the northeast. "White men," he signed.

The breed turned to Lassiter and addressed him in the birdlike gibberish the whites called a language. Brule had tried to learn the tongue, but found the chirpings almost impossible to duplicate. He knew a few words—that was all.

Lassiter moved to the edge of the shelf and studied the smoke a while. He then employed sign to say to Brule, "I think you are right. No Indian would make a fire that gave off so much smoke. Sneak down there and see how many there are. We will wait here for you."

Brule saw Cano go to speak and quickly jogged

off. He suspected that the breed wanted to go along but he would much rather scout by himself.

Perhaps because of his Indian blood, Cano liked to spend time with Brule, a feeling the Blood did not reciprocate. He came to a game trail and flew toward the grassy basin below, making as little sound as the wind itself.

The smoke rose from fir trees near the mouth of the valley, which was watered by a stream large enough to contain beaver. Brule soon spied a beaver lodge, leading him to suspect the fire had been made by trappers.

He heard their voices long before he glimpsed the camp, which was typical. Brule didn't know why, but white men always raised their voices much higher than they needed to. It was as if they were taught at an early age to bellow instead of to speak in normal tones. They talked loudly, they laughed loudly, they snored loudly—all in keeping with the loathsome creatures they were.

Brule slowed and flitted from tree to tree. Presently he saw a string of horses, eight in all. The fire blazed in the middle of a clearing. A lean-to had been erected, and under it sat a beefy man sharpening a knife on a whetstone. Two other men were by the fire, sipping coffee.

Going prone, Brule snaked to a bush at the clearing's edge. From there he spied a pile of steel traps beside the lean-to. He counted three rifles and five pistols between them.

But it was the knife that interested Brule most of all. It was extraordinary, at least three hands long, the blade sharp on both sides instead of just one, the hilt a glorious golden hue and encrusted with several sparkling stones. Brule's breath caught in his throat as he marveled at its beauty. It was unlike any knife he had ever seen, and he wanted it so badly that he tingled in anticipation.

There was only one problem.

When it came to plunder, Lassiter had the final say. Spoils were always collected into a heap and passed out as Lassiter saw fit. If any of them wanted a particular item, they were free to say so. Usually Lassiter handed it over, but not always. Brule had lost a fine red blanket and an ax he coveted to Cano.

This time would be different. Brule was not about to let anyone else lay claim to the magnificent knife owned by the beefy trapper. He would take it for himself and slay anyone who objected.

In order to have first claim, Brule knew he had to dispose of the whites himself. With the thought came action. There was no hesitation, no prick of conscience. Whites were his enemies. Enemies were to be slain. Life was as simple as that.

Brule backed into the trees and made like an eel, worming his way around the camp perimeter until he was behind the lean-to. It would have been better to wait until dark, but nightfall was hours off and Lassiter was bound to come see what was taking him so long.

The Blood placed his rifle on the ground and drew both his slender knife and the steel tomahawk. Rising into a crouch, he stalked to the side of the lean-to and peeked around the corner. One of the whites at the fire had his back to Brule; the other was busy refilling the coffeepot. The man in the lean-to was bent low, stroking that grand knife with delicate precision.

Brule's pulse quickened at being so close to the unique weapon. Its gleaming brilliance dazzled him. He had to restrain a mad impulse to dash over and snatch the knife from the man's hand.

The trappers by the fire owned rifles, which were propped on a nearby saddle. One had a pair of flintlocks, the other a single pistol. The man in the lean-to also possessed a rifle but it had carelessly been leaned against a sapling in front of the shelter. He also had two pistols under his belt.

Coiling his legs, Brule cast about for an object to throw and found a small stone that suited his purpose. Transferring the tomahawk to his left hand, he hurled the stone as far as he could into the firs on the opposite side of the clearing. It hit a high branch, then clattered earthward from limb to limb until it thudded on the ground.

Both trappers at the fire stood and warily peered into the trees. The man who owned the wonderful knife looked up from the whetstone.

In that moment when they were distracted, Brule struck. He was on the beefy man before the white could blink. His tomahawk cleaved the air and the man's skull with equal ease, shearing deep into the brain. The man died without an outcry, blood spurting from the rupture.

Without hesitation Brule whirled and charged the other pair. They both had heard the blow and turned. The nearest was momentarily paralyzed with fright but at last made a grab for a flintlock. By then Brule was close enough to throw his knife with an accuracy honed by years of practice.

The slim blade imbedded itself in the base of the man's throat. Squealing, the trapper clutched in a panic at the hilt and wrenched. The blade popped free. A scarlet geyser followed it, pouring onto the grass at the man's feet.

Brule didn't give the man another look. He concentrated on reaching the last trapper before the white man could draw a pistol. His arm arched in an overhand blow that brought the tomahawk streaking down at the trapper's head but the man was too fast for him and dodged aside while simultaneously drawing a flintlock.

Spinning, Brule slashed sideways. The tomahawk clipped the pistol a glancing blow, just enough to deflect the barrel at the very instant the man squeezed the trigger. There was a loud blast and the ball went wide.

The trapper speared a hand at his other pistol. Brule leaped in close and swung again. This time he connected, but not with the man's face, as he wanted. The tomahawk's keen edge bit into the trapper's arm above the wrist and sliced the hand clean off.

Uttering a scream of pure terror, the last trapper tried to flee. Brule was on the man in two bounds. He swung the tomahawk a final time and was splattered with gore when it split the trapper's head like a soft melon. The man pitched forward, limp and lifeless.

Brule turned to check on the one he had wounded in the jugular. The man had tottered a few feet toward the horses and fallen to his knees. Blood gushed and gushed, soaking the trapper's buckskins and the soil. Brule stepped over and raised the tomahawk on high.

The trapper twisted, eyes wide in stark terror. He managed to croak a few words in his strange tongue, red spittle flecking his lips.

There was a loud crunch as the tomahawk split the man's forehead wide open. Brule let the white man sag, then braced a foot on his chest and tugged on the haft. The blade came loose with a sucking sound.

Brule had to work swiftly. He wiped the tomahawk clean on the dead man's leggings, then tucked it under his own. A glance at the shelf showed Lassiter and the rest galloping down the slope, drawn by the shot.

Quickly Brule dashed to the lean-to and claimed his prize. The blade gleamed brightly; the bejeweled hilt sparkled and shimmered. Brule stripped the bearded man of a large sheath, discarded his own, and strapped on the new one. Into it he slid his new weapon.

Taking his old knife in hand, Brule scalped the former owner. In turn, he scalped the other two, and was just rising with all three dripping trophies in hand when Earl Lassiter rode into the clearing and drew rein.

The men muttered among themselves. Cano appeared most displeased. Lassiter looked around, a scowl indicating his state of mind.

"It would have been better if you had waited for us."

Brule ignored the remark, delivered in curt sign. Discarding the old knife, he hastened around behind the lean-to and retrieved his rifle. Only when he could shoot the first one who lifted a finger against him did he swing toward the angry men.

"I wanted you to wait," Lassiter signed.

Brule deposited the scalps on the lean-to so he could respond. "I had to kill them," he signed.

"Did they spot you?" Lassiter asked.

"No," Brule signed.

"Did they hear you then?" Lassiter asked. "Why did you have to slay them?"

To answer honestly would invite trouble, so Brule elected not to reply. Instead he stuffed the scalps into a parfleche he carried slung over his chest. The whites took to chattering like chipmunks, snapping at one another. It was clear they were extremely upset. He observed them on the sly, ready to defend himself if need be.

Eventually Lassiter shrugged and pointed at the rifles and pistols belonging to the trappers, then at the packs. Everyone dismounted except the breed and commenced sorting through the plunder.

Brule came out from behind the lean-to and watched. He had no interest in the booty. He already had the only item he wanted.

Just then Cano kneed his bay closer and stared hard at Brule's waist. He said something that aroused the interest of all the whites.

"Where did you get that knife?" Lassiter signed.

Again Brule chose not to reply. He would not let Lassiter lord it over him. He was free to do as he wanted whenever he wanted, and he was accountable to no man, least of all a white man.

Cano chirped at the others, using many angry gestures. Bear spoke, then Dixon. Cano shook his head, growing madder and madder. At length he addressed Lassiter and the two of them argued for a minute.

Brule could see that the breed was urging Lassiter to act but Lassiter appeared reluctant. He kept his own features as impassive as the smooth face of a cliff.

Earl Lassiter gazed at the new sheath, then at Brule. "The breed is upset and I do not blame him. As leader of this band, I have the right to pass out the spoils as I want to. And I promised him that he could have the first choice of weapons the next time. He has been wanting a new rifle for some time."

"I did not take a rifle," Brule signed.

"I know," Lassiter signed. "But you did take that knife. And now Cano wants it." He paused and mustered a patently fake smile. "So why not make everyone happy and give it to him? You can always get another later."

"I want this one."

"Have you been paying attention? Cano wants it too. And since he has every right to it, I am afraid you have no choice but to hand it over."

"There is one other choice."

"Which is?" Lassiter asked.

Brule's answer was to snap his rifle up and plant a ball smack between Cano's greedy eyes.

Chapter Six

Nate King had to hand it to Bill Zeigler. The old trapper had guided them unerringly over some of the roughest terrain in the mountains to the valley where Jeremiah Sawyer lived with his Crow wife.

Old Bill had done it all from memory. He knew the location of every prominent peak, pass, mountain, and vale. He'd tell them to be on the lookout for such and such a landmark, and sure enough, they'd spot it just when he said they should.

"Now look for some pines to the north," Zeigler said as they entered the valley. "His lodge will be there."

Zach poked a finger in the air. "Over yonder are a bunch of pines. Want me to go on ahead, Pa, and let Mr. Sawyer know we're coming?" He had met Jeremiah Sawyer on several occasions and rated him the nicest trapper in the Rockies next to his own father. He was also quite fond of Sawyer's oldest daughter, Beth, and couldn't wait to see her again.

"Go ahead, son," Nate said. "Just hail the lodge before you go riding up to it so Jeremiah doesn't mistake you for a Blackfoot."

Giddy with excitement, Zach galloped toward the pines. He sorely missed having others his age to be with. If there was any one drawback to living in the mountains, it was the lack of company that came calling and the all-too-few times the family went visiting.

During the summer they always spent time with the Shoshones, and Zach loved every minute of it. He was half Indian, after all. His mother's culture was part and parcel of his being. Except for his blue eyes, which he got from his pa, he could pass for a Shoshone anywhere, anytime.

To Zach's regret, he'd had little to do with his father's people. Trappers, yes, but they were hardly typical of the people back in the States, as his father had pointed out many times. Nate kept promising that one day they would make the long trek to New York City so Zach could see where his pa had been born and bred, but so far an opportunity hadn't presented itself.

Beth Sawyer had often expressed the same wish. She yearned to visit the States, to see how folks back there lived. Zach and her had talked it over endlessly.

Now, as Zach came to a clearing, he beamed happily, eager for a glimpse of Beth. But all he saw was the charred ruin of a lodge. Shocked, he reined up.

Somewhere, sparrows twittered. In the distance

a hawk screeched. All Zach had eyes and ears for was the clearing. Nudging the paint forward, he stopped beside a stump and slid down.

Zach had seen similar sights too many times in his brief life. He swallowed a lump that formed in his throat as he imagined sweet Beth and her younger sister, Claire, being brutally slain by hostiles.

The soft tread of a stealthy footstep behind Zach made him realize his mistake. Instead of staying alert he had permitted his mind to drift. Fearing he was about to be killed by those responsible for the deaths of the Sawyers, he spun, or tried to. He wasn't halfway around when something slammed into the middle of his back, knocking him onto his hands and knee.

Racked by pain, Zach nonetheless threw himself to the right, rolling onto his back and making a play for the pistol his father had given him for his last birthday.

Zach's hand had barely closed on the smooth wood butt when a foot rammed into his sternum. The breath whooshed from his lungs. For a few seconds his vision spun. When it cleared, he found himself staring up at an awful apparition that resembled a man he knew and respected.

It was Jeremiah Sawyer. A leather patch covered his left eye, attached by a thong looped around his head, while his right eye blazed with inner light. His hair was disheveled and matted with dirt. A deep scar marred his left cheek. In his hands he held a wooden club. His leggings were torn, his moccasins in tatters, and there was a bullet hole in his left thigh.

"Mr. Sawyer?" Zach croaked. "It's me, sir.

Zachary King. Don't you remember me?"

The man whom Zach felt was most like his own father blinked and slowly lowered the club. "Zach?" he rasped, his skin pallid. "Is that really you, boy?"

"Yes, sir," Zach said, wheezing as he tried to breathe again. "My folks are with me too. Are you all right, sir?"

"All right?" Jeremiah said and did an odd thing. He laughed long and loud, a strident, wavering sort of laugh that no normal person would ever make.

The crash of horses coming through the brush emboldened Zach to sit up. He saw the stunned disquiet on the faces of his folks and thought he should explain. "I forgot to hail. He didn't know it was me."

Nate merely nodded. He could see his son was unharmed. Sliding from the stallion, he stared at the blackened circle where the lodge had stood and beyond it at three graves crowned by crude crosses. The very calamity that he had always dreaded would strike his own family had felled that of his good friend. He put a hand on Sawyer's shoulder. "Jeremiah?"

The other man averted his sole eye and voiced a low, pathetic whine. He coughed a few times, then looked up, his haggard features a shadow of their former healthy hue. "Nice to see you again, Nate."

"Have a seat," Nate said. "We'll fix coffee and a bite to eat. You look half starved."

"I reckon I am," Jeremiah said. He sank onto the stump and placed the club between his legs. "I can't quite recollect when I ate a full meal last.

I know it's been two weeks or better since—" He broke off to swallow and lick his lips.

"If you'd rather not talk about it, that's fine," Nate said. "For now, just rest."

Winona and Old Bill had climbed from their horses. Sawyer seemed not to notice them. His good eye fixed on something in the distance, something only he could see. "It's never enough, is it?" he said softly. "No matter how hard we try, it's never enough."

"How do you mean?" Nate asked, but received no response. He exchanged knowing glances with Winona, who gave the cradleboard to Zach so she could get a fire going that much sooner.

Old Bill squatted by the stump. "Jeremiah? It's me, your good pard. Don't you recognize me?"

Sawyer blinked a few times. "Bill? You're here too? Well, isn't this something? All my friends are showing up. How did you hear?"

"Hear?"

"About my wife and my precious sweethearts? About the murdering sons of bitches who killed them and nearly killed me. I'm going to get them, Bill. You watch. No matter how long it takes, no matter what I have to do, I'm going to find them and make them pay." Jeremiah absently turned toward the horses and gave a start. "Look! Just what I need! Did you bring them for me? I can't thank you enough."

The next instant the apparition was on his feet, stepping toward the stallion.

"If you want to tag along, you're welcome. But we're not stopping until we find them. We'll eat in the saddle, sleep in the saddle. If the horses drop dead, we'll find others."

Nate darted between his friend and the animals. "Hold on, Jeremiah," he said kindly, putting a hand on the man's chest. "You're not going anywhere right this minute. You need food; you need some sleep. And we have to talk."

Sawyer's features clouded and his spine went rigid. "Get out of my way, Nate. I can't afford any more delays. Those butchers have a lot to answer for."

"You're not leaving," Nate said.

It was as plain as the nose on his face that his friend was extremely upset, so he expected to get an argument. What he didn't expect was for Sawyer to haul off and take a swing at him. If Jeremiah hadn't been so weak he could hardly stand, the blow would have felled Nate like a poled ox. As it was, the punch clipped Nate's chin and made him recoil a step to ward off several other blows.

But then the punches stopped. The effort crumpled Jeremiah Sawyer in his tracks. Venting a loud groan, he feebly tried to rise, his once powerful arms trembling violently from the strain.

"No!" Jeremiah wailed. "You have to let me go! Those bastards have to pay!" Moisture rimming his eye, he tried to stand. He looked up at Nate in eloquent appeal but Nate made no move to help him. Scowling, he glanced at Zach. "Please, Zachary. They killed Beth! You liked her, didn't you? Don't you want to see her killers punished?"

Torn by turmoil, Zachary started to go to the man's aid, but drew up short at a gesture from his father.

"Winona!" Sawyer said. "Bill!"

Neither of them moved.

"Damn it all!" Jeremiah raged at Nate. "If it had been your family, you know I'd help you!"

"We'll lend a hand, but we'll do it right," Nate said. Hooking his arm under Sawyer's, he hoisted Jeremiah onto the stump and steadied him until he could sit up straight unassisted. "How long ago did this happen?"

"I told you. About two weeks, I think," Jeremiah said. "I've lost track of time." Slumping, he bowed his forehead to his left knee. His next words were barely audible. "It's a miracle I'm still alive, old friend. I remember running, with them nipping at my heels like a pack of rabid wolves. A shot hit me in the leg, and I thought for sure it was all over. Then I came to a ravine north of here." Jeremiah paused, his voice breaking. "I was looking for a way down when I turned to see how close they were and a ball caught me in the eye. That's the last I recollect for quite a spell."

There were so many questions Nate wanted to ask, but his friend was too worn down. He stripped his bedroll off the stallion and spread it out. "Here. Catch up on your rest."

This time Sawyer didn't object. He slid onto the blankets and lay on his back. "I've been sleeping on the ground for so long I'd forgotten how soft a blanket can feel."

Winona had a fire going. She filled their coffeepot with water, then took a small bundle of herbs from a parfleche and added three slivers of root about the size of a large coin. "Toza," she said when she noticed Sawyer looking at her. "It is the root of a plant quite common in these mountains. When dug up, it resembles a carrot in shape, but smells and tastes like the celery I once tasted when my husband took me to New Orleans years ago."

"What does it do?"

"Toza is a tonic. It will help you build up your strength quickly."

"It better. I don't care what your husband says. Once I'm strong enough, I'm leaving."

Winona remembered Sawyer as a man whose poise had never been ruffled, not by wild beasts, not by enemy tribes, not by anything. It was said that Jeremiah Sawyer always kept his head, even in the midst of dire crisis.

This was a gravely different man. The deaths of his loved ones had pushed him close to the brink of mental chaos. Winona sensed it wouldn't take much to drive him over that brink, and then there was no telling what he might do.

Young Zachary stood close by, watching the man he thought he knew. Like his mother, he recognized that something was terribly wrong inside of the man's head. He wondered if Jeremiah would ever be the same carefree man he had always been. Somehow, Zach doubted it. Glancing up, he saw his father walk over to the graves.

Nate was even more troubled than his wife and son. Had circumstances been different, the situation might have been reversed. Would he burn for vengeance as his friend did? he asked himself. And being an honest man, he admitted that he would. The murder of a man's family was the one atrocity he could never forgive or forget.

Many times Nate had lain awake at night, fretting the same fate might befall those he cared for. Violent death was part and parcel of wilderness existence, but acknowledging the fact didn't make the reality any easier to bear.

Old Bill Zeigler ambled over. "I think he's driftin' off," he whispered. "Let's hope so. Sleep would do him a world of good."

"And make him harder to handle if he decides to ride out on us," Nate said.

"You can't blame him," Old Bill said. He rubbed the stubble on his chin, his brow knitting. "Say, do you reckon that the same bunch that rubbed out Buffalo Hump are the ones who paid Jeremiah a visit?"

In the tragedy of the moment, Nate had completely forgotten about the reason for their visit. "Could be," he said and checked an urge to question Sawyer more. He would just have to wait until the man was in better shape.

"If so, that means they're drifting north," Old Bill said. "I don't like that one bit. Go north far enough and we'll hit Blackfoot country."

"Maybe the ones we're after are Blackfeet," Nate said.

"I doubt it," Old Bill said. "Blackfeet may be a lot of things, but they ain't lazy. When they set about wipin' a family out, they generally do a thorough job. If they saw Jeremiah fall into a ravine, they'd climb down to be damn certain he was dead and to lift his hair."

"Maybe the ravine was too steep."

"For Blackfeet? You know as well as I do that they can climb like mountain sheep when they set their minds to it," Old Bill said. "No, if you ask me, whoever did this was a mite sloppy. And we both know Indians ain't ever sloppy."

Nate was about to go to the fire when he saw that small letters had been carved on the dead branches used to make the crosses. Hunkering down, he read the first inscription aloud. "Here lies my darling wife, Yellow Flower. My soul died with you."

"Damn," Old Bill said.

"In memory of Bethany Sawyer," Nate said, reading the second. "She met her Maker before her time."

"It must have taken him days to carve all them words."

The last was the hardest to read. The letters were fainter, as if Sawyer had become too weak to wield the knife effectively. "Here lies little Claire Sawyer," Nate read, "whose only sin was being born."

The old mountain man leaned down to run his fingers across the words. "Pitiful, ain't it? But that's the way life is sometimes. Just when we think we have it licked, it tears our innards out."

"Is that experience speaking?" Nate asked idly.

"What else? When you've lived as long as I have, you learn a thing or three." Old Bill adopted a melancholy air and raised his hand to touch below both eyes. "When I was your age, King, I was a regular hellion. Now look at me. I never figured on ending my days as blind as bat, of no use to anyone, not even myself."

"You're of use to me," Nate said. "You know this neck of the country much better than I do."

"So what? I can hardly get around by myself anymore. If you hadn't come along when you did, I'd still be stuck in my little valley, blunderin' around, trying to live off the land as best I could, knowin' damn well that sooner or later a bear or a painter or somethin' else would come along and make wolf meat of me."

"Yet you stayed on."

"What else was I to do?" Old Bill said bitterly. Turning, he walked off before he made a mistake and gave King a clue to his real motivation in tagging along. He saw the boy unsaddling the horses and joined him. "I'll unsaddle my own."

Zachary, downcast, merely nodded.

"Cat got your tongue?" Old Bill asked.

"I knew his daughters really well," Zach said, indicating Sawyer, who was sound asleep.

"That's death for you." Zeigler gripped the cinch.

"How can you be so coldhearted about it?" Zachary asked. "Didn't you know this family?"

"I did," Old Bill said. "But when you have as many gray hairs as I do, you know that death can strike anyone at any time. Few of us have any say over when and where we'll pass on. It's like rollin' a pair of dice. You never know what will come up."

"I hope I get to chose."

Old Bill smirked. "You and me both, son. You and me both."

In due course the animals were bedded down for the night, Zachary and Zeigler had filled the water skins, and Winona had fixed rabbit stew, courtesy of a fine shot Nate made. Jeremiah Sawyer slept the whole time, until hours after the sun had set.

Nate was sipping a delicious cup of coffee when he heard Jeremiah groan. The man had been tossing and turning ever since he'd fallen asleep, occasionally muttering incoherently. Twice he had cried out, an animal cry of sheer torment, but he had not awakened.

Now Nate saw Jeremiah's face contort into an agonized mask. Jeremiah rolled onto his right side, then back onto his left. His fingers clenched and unclenched as if he were throttling someone in his dreams. His teeth gnashed together so loud it sounded like metal grinding on metal. He started mumbling, the words growing louder and louder.

"I'll save you! I'll save you, girls! No one will hurt you! No one will harm your mother!"

Zachary listened with bated breath from across the fire. "Should we wake him, Pa?"

"No," Nate said, aware that sometimes those in the grip of terrible nightmares lashed out at anyone who tried to bring them around. "We'll wait a bit."

Jeremiah flipped onto his back. He made tiny mewling sounds, like those a frightened kitten might make. Next his mouth worked but no words came out. His hands rose to his throat and he sucked in air as if drowning. Eyelids quivering, he shook from head to toe.

"Are you sure he's not dying?" Zach asked.

As if in answer, Jeremiah sat bolt upright, his eye the size of a walnut, his face slick with sweat. He gazed into the night, his jaw muscles twitching, his hands shaking convulsively. "I'm coming, dearest!" he wailed. "Wait for me! I'm coming!" Propping both palms under him, he went to rise.

Nate guessed Sawyer's intent and intercepted him. Jeremiah took but a single step when Nate seized him around the shoulders and coaxed him toward the blankets. "Easy there, friend. You not going anywhere in the shape you're in."

Jeremiah motioned at the inky forest. "What are you doing? Can't you hear her?"

"Who?" Nate asked while attempting to ease him down.

Sawyer resisted, pushing weakly at his chest. "Yellow Flower! There! See her!" Jeremiah pointed, aglow with excitement. "She's still alive! I only thought she was dead! Please let me go to her!"

"I can't," Nate said.

"You must!" Jeremiah had worked himself into a fever pitch of desperation. He lunged, shoving hard, but Nate held firm. "What kind of pard are you? She needs me. Damn it!"

"Calm down!"

Nate might as well have railed at the wind. Jeremiah struggled fiercely, a virtual madman. What he lacked in brute force he made up for in devilish cunning. He raked at Nate's eyes with his fingernails, and when Nate raised his arms to deflect the blow, Jeremiah jumped to the left to scoot around him.

From two sides Winona and Old Bill closed in. They snared Jeremiah between them and held fast. He kicked and shouted and cursed until he was too weak to open his mouth. As they lowered him down, he burst into tears of abject misery, burying his face in the blankets.

"Will he ever be his old self again, Pa?" Zachary whispered.

"There's no telling," Nate asked. "When a man's spirit is broken, he can lose the will to live."

"Mr. Sawyer is no quitter. He'll be as good as new before too long."

The boy's confidence seemed misplaced to Nate but he held his tongue and was glad he did. For the very next morning he awoke to the uncomfortable feeling that he was being watched, and when he rose on an elbow, he discovered his intuition hadn't failed him.

All the others were sleeping, except for Jeremiah, who had his back supported by the stump and was regarding the brightening sky with intense interest. "Good morning," he said, sounding more like his old self. "Before you say a word, I want to apologize for yesterday. I don't quite recollect everything that happened, but I know I wasn't myself and that I gave you a hard time."

"How are you feeling now?"

"Just dandy," Jeremiah said. "Fit enough to ride. I'd be obliged if you'd let me have one of your horses. I'll get it back to you as soon as I can."

"When we leave, we leave together. I have a hunch we're after the same men you are," Nate said and related the pertinent facts about Buffalo Hump and the Utes.

"It could be the same outfit," Jeremiah said. "If it is, we're better off working together. There are seven of them, every man as mean as a rabid dog."

From a few yards away Bill Zeigler's voice piped up. "You can count me in. I know that I only offered to act as your guide until we got here, but I wouldn't miss this frolic for the world."

Nate King glanced from one to the other. He had deep doubts about taking them. Sawyer's quest for vengeance might endanger them all. And Zeigler couldn't hit the broad side of a barn at 20 feet. Relying on either could prove disastrous.

Refusing both was the logical thing to do. Logic, however, was no match for the one emotion that makes a man do things time and again against his better judgment.

Nate looked at his wife and children. The odds being what they were, he needed all the help he could get. "Fair enough. We ride together."

Old Bill chuckled. "Now the real fun starts."

Chapter Seven

Earl Lassiter wasn't in the best of moods. For one thing, he'd lost a fine tracker and interpreter when Cano's brains were blown out by the Blood. For another, his men were growing more and more restless as they traveled farther and farther north. If they didn't find some plump pilgrims to pluck soon, Dixon and Bear might see fit to strike off on their own.

Holding a bunch of callous killers together for any length of time had proven more trying than Lassiter counted on. There were countless petty squabbles to be handled, days on end when one or the other was in a foul temper and as likely to kill one of their own as anyone else.

The business with Cano had only made matters worse. None of his men cared for the Blood but they had all accepted the breed, more or less, because the breed had some white blood in his veins.

After Cano's death, there had been muttering behind Brule's back. Bear had come right out and said they should do to Brule as he had done to Cano.

Lassiter was inclined to agree. But he couldn't lay a finger on the Blood, nor allow anyone else to do so, until they found someone to replace him, which wouldn't be that simple. Warriors from friendly tribes weren't about to join his band. And warriors from hostile tribes would rather kill them than join.

Hooking up with Brule had been a once in a lifetime fluke, and at first Lassiter had been elated. The Blood was more deadly than a grizzly, more silent than a stalking mountain lion, more brutal than an enraged wolverine. He was the perfect killer, and Lassiter had been thrilled at having him on a short leash.

Now Lassiter knew otherwise. He no longer trusted the Blood. When they were together, Lassiter never turned his back to him. Brule was like a coiled sidewinder, set to strike at the slightest provocation.

Such was the train of thought that occupied Lassiter as he wound down a switchback to a ridge that overlooked a tableland to the north. He heard his name mentioned and looked around.

"Are you deaf?" Dixon asked. "I wanted to know how much farther you think it is?"

"You'll find out when we get there," Lassiter said gruffly, then remembered that he had to keep in Dixon's good graces or he would lose the man. He extended his arm to the northeast. "About a day's ride, I think. If I'm right, South Pass is that way. The wagons come over the pass and make straight for the Green River Valley. Somewhere between the two we should strike paydirt."

"You hope," Dixon said.

"He's not the only one," Ben Kingslow said. "I wouldn't mind having a few dollars in my pocket for a change. After we get this over with, maybe we can head east to the nearest fort. I want to get so drunk I can't stand up."

"We can't go to no fort," Snip said. "We'd be shot on the spot."

"Why, pray tell?" Kingslow asked.

"Have you forgotten what we did to that old Injun and his daughters? And that stubborn cuss and his family? And those three trappers Brule wiped out? Hell, man. Every mountaineer this side of the Rockies must be looking for us."

Ben Kingslow laughed. Of them all, Bear was the densest between the ears, but Snip had his moments. "No one is after us for those killings because no one knows we're to blame," he said. "So long as we keep covering our tracks, we'll be fine."

"Which is why we never leave witnesses," Lassiter said. "Kids, women—you name it. If they see us, they die."

"I don't much like killing sprouts," Bear said.

"Would you rather they squawked and Bridger or McNair came after us?" Lassiter said. "You know as well as I do that neither of those uppity sons of bitches would stand for having a pack of killers on the loose. They'd round up as many men as they needed and stay on our trail until hell froze over or they caught us."

"I don't want that," Bear said, "but I still don't like putting holes in kids. My mama raised me better than that."

Bear was sincere, which made it all the harder for him to understand why the rest of his friends burst into rollicking waves of laughter. "What did I say?" he asked when the mirth tapered off. It provoked another round of mirth.

Annoyed, Bear slapped his big legs against his mount and began to ride past Lassiter. Because he was glaring at the others and not watching where he was going, he nearly rode into the finely muscled figure blocking the way. He reined up in the nick of time.

Instantly the laughter ceased. Lassiter advanced, trying not to let his true feelings show. He resorted to sign language. "Have you found the trail, Brule?"

The Blood's fingers flew. "Yes. Far ahead. I have also found three wagons. There are three whites in the first, four in the second, only two in the third. Six are adults, the rest children. They travel very slowly."

Overjoyed, Lassiter yipped like a coyote, then relayed the news to his men. Only Kingslow also knew the universal hand language of the Indians. "How long will it take us to get there?" Lassiter asked the stoic warrior.

"You will be at the trail before the sun touches the horizon."

Lassiter thought fast. "No, we won't. I can't risk giving ourselves away before the time comes to pay those pilgrims a visit. Find us a good spot to camp for the night. Tomorrow we'll start stalking them."

"As you wish."

"I knew our luck would hold," Lassiter told his eager listeners. "We'll shadow them for a day or two, then help ourselves."

"To the women too?" Dixon asked and smacked his lips hungrily.

"To whatever the hell you want."

Her name was Katie Brandt and she was in love. In love with her husband of only six months, in love with the vast prairie and the regal mountains, in love with the bold notion of venturing to Oregon Country, where few had gone before, and in love with life itself.

On this day she sat beside Glen on the high seat of their creaking schooner and smiled as a yellow butterfly flew past. In front of their team of plodding oxen were two more wagons, the foremost driven by the Ringcrest family, the second the property of the Potters.

"What a grand and glorious adventure this is," Katie said breathlessly. "I'm so happy that I let you talk me into making this journey."

Her handsome husband arched an eyebrow at her. "Oh? For a while there, I thought you would pack your bags and go back east to your folks before you'd set foot past the Mississippi."

"I'm sorry I was so stubborn," Katie said. "I just didn't want to lose you so soon after tying the knot." She had made no secret of her fear. And who could blame her? The tales told about the savages that populated the wilderness were enough to turn a peaceful person's hair white.

"How do you feel now that you've learned all your fretting was for nothing?" Glen asked.

"Like a fool for acting so silly," Katie said. "But need I remind you that we're not out of the woods yet? It's many hundreds of miles to Oregon Country."

"Always optimistic, aren't you, dearest?" Glen said. "I keep telling you that the route we're taking doesn't pass through the territory of a single hostile tribe, but you won't listen."

"Only because I happen to know that hostile tribes like the Blackfeet roam anywhere they so please. We're in Shoshone territory now, but that doesn't mean we won't run into a Blackfoot war party."

Glen laughed. "And here I thought you had a sunny disposition. If I'd known you always looked at the dark side of things, I might never have proposed."

"Is that a fact?" Katie grinned and gave her man a playful smack on the shoulder.

Laughing, Glen Brandt clucked at the oxen. His cheerful demeanor hid a constant gnawing worry. For the truth was that he shared his wife's concern. They were taking a great risk making the trip, so great that he had debated with himself for weeks before committing himself. Many Oregon-bound travelers had lost their lives on the perilous journey and he didn't want his lovely wife to share their horrid fate.

Glen felt confident they would make it though. It was spring, and at that time of the year, the Blackfeet usually stayed close to their own region, busy hunting and stockpiling jerky and pemmican after the long, hard winter.

Plus their small caravan was being led by a man who had made the trip on horseback once before.

Peter Ringcrest had gone to the Pacific Northwest some years ago with Dr. Marcus Whitman's party. Whitman had been sent by the American Board of Commissioners of Foreign Missions to learn whether the Nez Perce and Flatheads tribes were receptive to missionary work. Once they established the Indians would accept them with open arms, Ringcrest had hastened back to the States to fetch his wife and son and anyone else who wanted to go along.

To hear Peter Ringcrest tell it, the Oregon Country justly deserved its reputation as the Promised Land. A mild climate, abundant rainfall, and rich soil made it a paradise for those who eked their living from the earth. Astoria and other growing communities afforded promise to those whose bent was more toward town life. And already the verdant forests were being tapped for their vast reserves of lumber.

"Oregon is heaven on earth!" Ringcrest liked to exclaim, and Glen believed him. He couldn't wait to stake a claim to a choice parcel and build a house that would do his wife proud. Not just any old dwelling or rustic cabin would suffice for the woman he loved.

"Oh, look," Katie said, giggling. "They're at it again."

Glen glanced at the back of the Potter wagon, where the two girls, Tricia and Agatha, were making faces at them. Agatha scrunched up her lively features and stuck out her tongue so Glen did the same. Both girls went into hysterics.

"Aren't they little darlings." Katie sighed. "I can't wait to have a girl of our very own."

"I'm partial to the notion of a son, myself,"

Glen said. "That way, when he's older, he can help out around the farm. Three or four boys would be even better. They could handle most of the chores and give us more time to ourselves."

"Three or four?" Katie said. "How many children would you like to have?"

"Oh, I don't know," Glen said, keeping an eye on a large rock close to the rutted track. He didn't want to break a wheel so early in the journey. "Maybe nine or ten, like my pa had."

"I think we had better sit down tonight and have us a long talk. I like the idea of a large family too, but my idea of large is four or five at the most."

They debated the issue then and there while the sun climbed steadily higher. Toward noon they stopped, as was their custom, in a shaded glade watered by a spring. The oxen were let loose from harness, and the horses tied to the first and third wagons were likewise allowed to drink and graze.

Katie spread out a blanket under a cottonwood and had a small meal waiting for Glen when he was done with the stock. The other couples were similarly occupied nearby. The Potter girls and the Ringcrest boy scampered about like chipmunks, whooping and hollering.

"Isn't life wonderful?" Katie said before taking a bite from a sweetmeat.

"So long as I'm with you, it is," Glen said, folding her free hand in his.

Katie brazenly pecked him on the cheek. As she straightened, her gaze happened to stray to the thickly clustered trees beyond the spring. A patch of brown in the midst of the green foliage piqued her curiosity. For a few moments she studied it.

Then the outline solidified and she gasped, unable to credit her own eyes.

"What's the matter?" Glen asked.

Startled so that she was unable to speak, Katie tried to vent a scream. A chill coursed down her spine, immobilizing her. She could see the cruel face clearly. The man's dark, fearsome eyes bored into hers as if into the depths of her soul.

Glen was sitting up. "What the dickens is it?" he asked and began to turn to look for himself.

The abominable face vanished. Katie leaped to her feet and screeched, clutching herself to keep from shivering. She felt Glen grip her arms and heard their friends running up. Even the children came, cowed into timid silence.

Peter Ringcrest was the first to speak. "What's wrong?" he asked urgently, his rifle in hand. "Why did you cry out, Mrs. Brandt?"

Willing her hand to extend, Katie pointed at the spot. "I saw someone there. An Indian, I think. He was watching us." She paused, the chill spreading. "You should have seen his dreadful eyes! He was a hostile. I just know it!"

Glen grabbed his rifle. "I'll go look."

"No!" Peter Ringcrest said as he anxiously scoured the glade. "If there are hostiles, that's what they would want you to do so they can pick you off. Where would that leave your wife?"

"What do we do then?" Bob Potter asked. A tinker by trade, he was a thin, waspish man whose fear was thick enough to be cut by one of the knives he sharpened for a living.

"We get out of here while we still can," Ringcrest said. "Glen, you collect the oxen. Bob, the horses. Ladies, kindly load everything into the wagons.

We'll cut our stop short. Once we're out in the open, the hostiles won't be able to take us unawares."

The glade bustled with frantic activity. For once the children were quiet, meekly doing whatever they were told. In less than 15 minutes the wagons were rolling, the women handling the reins so the men would have their hands free to shoot if necessary.

No attack materialized. Katie wondered if she had imagined the whole thing, but on reflection she knew there had been a face, that it had been an Indian.

Once clear of the cottonwoods, the pilgrims breathed easier. Glen had been perched on the edge of the seat, cocked rifle in hand. He sat back and said, "Maybe we were lucky. Maybe there was just the one."

"What if he was a scout for a war party?" Katie asked.

"We'll play it safe from here on out," Glen said. "We'll stick to open country, no matter what. At night we'll take turns standing guard and keep a fire going at all times. If hostiles are dogging us, they might give up once they see we're ready for them."

"What if they don't?"

Glen locked his eyes on hers. "Then we won't get to have that big family after all."

"Three days," Earl Lassiter said. "Three stinking days and we haven't been able to make a move."

Ben Kingslow shrugged. "It ain't our fault that they're being so blamed careful. They're just cagier than most pilgrims."

"Damn them all to hell." Lassiter said. "I'll give it another day, two at the most. Then we're doing whatever it takes to wipe them out."

"Sure thing," Kingslow said, having learned long ago it was healthier to agree with anything and everything their leader said when Lassiter was in one of his foul moods.

This time around, Kingslow shared the same sentiments. He was weary to death of plodding along in the wake of the wagons, waiting for the golden opportunity to spring an ambush. But ever since leaving a glade many miles back, the pilgrims never once let down their guard. It made him wonder if they suspected that they were being followed, although he couldn't see how they had guessed.

The gang rode a full mile behind the wagons to keep from being seen. At night, Lassiter allowed a tiny fire only so long as it was well concealed. There was no way in hell, Kingslow reflected, that the pilgrims could have caught on, yet it appeared that they had.

A lithe form appeared, jogging tirelessly toward them.

"Here comes the stinking Blood again," Dixon said. "I wonder what he wants this time? It's still early afternoon. The pilgrims can't have stopped for the day already."

Lassiter reined up and awaited their scout. It bothered him that Brule had become more reticent than ever in recent days. The warrior still did as Lassiter wanted, but now he did so with a marked reluctance, leading Lassiter to suspect that the Blood planned to light out on his own some time soon.

All Lassiter asked was that Brule waited until after they hit the caravan. He'd sneaked a peek at the three wagons and was elated to learn they were heaped high with household possessions and other articles. It was his impassioned hope that one or two of the pilgrims carried a nest egg worth hundreds if not thousands of dollars.

If the latter, Lassiter planned to head east, back to the States, and use his ill-gotten grubstake to set himself up in business in New Orleans. He'd long harbored the notion of having his own gambling establishment or tavern. A few thousand were all he needed to make his dream come true.

Lassiter drew rein to await the Blood. Beside him Bear smacked his thick lips and wiped a grimy hand across his dirty face. "You need a bath," Lassiter said irritably.

"What for?" the giant asked. "It's not August."

"What does August have to do with anything?"

"That's the month I take my bath. My grandma used to say that anyone who takes more than one a year winds up sickly."

"I'd rather you were sickly than rank," Lassiter said and dropped the subject as the Blood halted in front of them. "What have you seen?" he signed.

"The whites have stopped at a stream and are making camp."

"Can we approach the camp without them seeing?"

"No. Again they have picked a spot that gives them a clear view in all directions. There are no trees, no brush, no boulders within shooting range. It is a spot they can easily defend. And again they park the wagons in a circle and string rope to keep their animals inside."

"Damn them!" Lassiter said aloud, then employed sign again. "Do you have any idea why they are stopping so soon? The sun will not set for a while yet."

"I could not get as close as I would have liked," Brule signed, "but it appears one of the little girls is ill. I saw her mother feeling her brow, as if for fever, and mopping her brow with a damp cloth."

"You have done well," Lassiter signed. "Keep a watch on them and inform me of anything new."

"I will."

After the warrior trotted off, Lassiter swung toward his men and relayed the news. "In a way this is a break for us. They'll go slower than ever with a sick brat on their hands. And sooner or later they're going to run out of open country. That's when we nail their hides to the wall."

"It better be soon," Dixon said. "I'm tired of holding back. Hell, Earl, there's six of us. Why don't we crawl up close to them in the dark and blast away? We might drop all the adults with the first volley."

"And if we don't?" Lassiter asked. "If just one of them gets away and somehow makes it to a fort?"

"It was just a thought," Dixon said.

Lassiter was tired of the man's ceaseless bellyaching. He half wished that Brule had shot Dixon instead of Cano, but then he would have been obliged to kill Brule on the spot. Abiding the death of a lowly breed was one thing; the death of a fellow white quite another.

They searched for half a mile to the north and south of the trail, but failed to find any water or a suitable place to take shelter for the night. Having no recourse, they bedded down in the open and made a cold camp.

Ben Kingslow munched on the last of his jerked buffalo meat and lamented the chain of events that had brought him to this low point in his life. A former trapper, and before that a holder of more jobs than he could shake a stick at, he had tired of working like a slave for a living and decided to take the easy way. Only it wasn't as easy as he'd thought it would be.

Bear slurped his coffee and thought of the women in those wagons. He couldn't wait to get his hands on them. Next to killing, the thing Bear liked most was to squeeze a soft female until she screamed.

Dixon sat by himself, his blue cap pulled low over his brow. He was tired of all the riding, tired of all the time they wasted when all they had to do was ride right up to the pilgrims, acting as innocent as could be, and then shoot them down when they lowered their guard.

Snip busied himself grooming his horse, a mare he had taken a fancy to.

Nearest the fire sat Lassiter. He decided to give it three more days. After that they would be too close to the Green River Valley, where many of the trappers congregated, to risk attacking the caravan. Three days it had to be. And then, come hell or high water, those damned pilgrims were going to die!

Chapter Eight

Jeremiah Sawyer practically crackled with impatience when he said, "Why have you stopped? I swear, King, you're slower than a snail. Can't you see that we're wasting precious time?"

Nate raised his head from the hoof he was examining. "Would you rather have one of our horses go lame?"

Instead of answering, Jeremiah glowered at the pack animal responsible for the delay, wheeled his mount, and rode ahead a score of yards to wait for the others.

Old Bill Zeigler sighed and shook his head. "That coon is as high strung as piano wire. He can't wait to get his hands on them who rubbed out his kin, and I can't say as how I blame him."

"Me neither," Nate said. "But you'd think he would be a little less touchy by now."

It had been six days since they had left the

valley Sawyer had once called home. From dawn to dusk they were in the saddle, except for brief stops when their horses needed rest.

Originally, they had followed a faint trail, indistinct tracks only Nate recognized as such. He was by far the better tracker, and thanks to him they had gained rapidly on the gang of cutthroats.

They also had the killers to thank. Apparently the gang had slain three trappers and lost one of their own in the bargain, a breed Sawyer recognized. The trapper's camp had been pillaged. From the amount of prints, and from the five empty whiskey bottles found scattered about the camp, Nate guessed that the killers had spent two days there, possibly more. A costly mistake.

Now the tracks were less than a day old and Nate knew that before too long he would at long last confront the callous butchers who stalked the land. The bloodthirsty fiends had to pay for slaying ten innocent people, and perhaps many more, and Nate was going to see that they did.

It was a confrontation Nate both relished and dreaded. He looked forward to putting an end to their reign of terror, but at the same time he was worried about his family and friends. The odds were such that not all of them would survive, not unless he was very, very careful.

That would be hard to do with Jeremiah Sawyer primed to explode at the first sight of those they sought. Nate had grown increasingly worried about his friend and keenly regretted giving Jeremiah the spare rifle he always packed along on long journeys.

These were the thoughts that filtered through Nate's head as he pulled his butcher knife and pried a small stone loose. Tossing the culprit aside, he lowered the pack animal's leg, gave it a pat on the neck, and stepped to the stallion.

Winona and Zach were talking in hushed tones. They stopped as Nate drew alongside them, and his wife spoke so that only he could hear, "We must talk."

Nate waved to Jeremiah, who resumed tracking with Old Bill as company. Once the pair were well beyond earshot, Nate brought the stallion to a brisk walk, riding so close to Winona that his stirrup brushed her foot. "So what's on your mind, as if I can't guess?"

"What are we going to do about him? He will get us all killed, the way he is acting."

"There's not much I can do. He won't listen to reason."

"Zach and I have an idea," Winona said, and their son nodded vigorously. "Tonight, after he falls asleep, we should jump him and tie him up. Between the four of us we can do it, even if he has regained his strength."

"And then what?" Nate asked. "We keep him trussed up until we've dealt with Lassiter and his bunch?"

"It would seem to be the smart thing to do," Winona said as crisply as ever. "Once we have done what must be done, we will cut him loose and all will be well."

"There are only two problems with that idea," Nate said. "One, we can't do it without him. There are six killers, one of them a full-blooded Blood according to Jeremiah. We're going to need all the help we can get."

"And the second problem?"

"He's liable to hold it against us if we tie him up until it's all over. You've seen the look that comes into his eyes now and again. He's as close to being a madman as a sane man can be and still claim sanity."

"We never should have brought him or old Bill along, husband."

Nate didn't care to be reminded of his mistake. Yet if he had to do it again, he would. His family came first, and with the two men along, he would be better able to protect them. He noticed the position of the sun, some two hours above the western horizon toward which they were headed.

Over a day and a half ago they had come on the grooved tracks of wagon wheels. "The trail to the Oregon Country," Nate had said while noting how the hoofprints of the killers swung westward, paralleling the trail. Initially he had been stumped. Were Lassiter and company heading for Oregon to escape retribution for their acts? Then he had realized that several wagons had passed by a short while before Lassiter's band reached the trail, and he was able to put two and two together.

The cutthroats were after the pilgrims in those wagons.

Nate had pushed the horses as hard as he dared until that very morning. To keep on doing so would exhaust them so badly the animals would be useless for days, in which case Lassiter would get clean away.

But Nate chafed at the delay as much as Jeremiah Sawyer. He looked up to see how far ahead the other two were and was surprised to see only Zeigler, galloping back toward them, and puffs of dust in the distance. "What's the matter?" he demanded as the older man came to a sliding halt.

"It's that danged Sawyer!" Old Bill said. "He's decided you're taking too damn long, so he's gone on ahead."

"He what?"

"I tried to talk him out of it. But he wouldn't listen. He said that he was tired of dragging his heels, that we could catch up when we wanted."

Exasperated beyond measure, Nate lifted his reins, then addressed Winona. "I'll go ahead and stop him. You take your time. There's no sense in running all our horses into the ground." He touched her elbow in parting and was off, the big black stallion responding superbly as it always did. A last glance was all he had of his loved ones; then he buckled down to the task of overtaking the lunatic who would ruin everything.

Fortunately the lay of the land was mostly level. To the north were rolling hills, to the south gullies and ravines. But the wagon trail itself was flat and open so Nate could let the stallion have its head without fear of a mishap.

Presently Nate spotted Jeremiah. Despite the distance, he could see the man flailing away at his mount with the reins, driving the animal relentlessly.

Slowly, the stallion narrowed the gap. The packhorse that Sawyer rode was no match for the black over a long haul. Nate smiled grimly to himself as he cut the yardage in half. Meanwhile, the sun arced into the blue sky. The shadows lengthened.

Jeremiah came to a grade and for the first time

looked back. On spying Nate, he renewed his efforts to spur his horse on. The animal faltered, but didn't go down.

Bent low over the stallion, Nate rode with the accomplished skill of a Comanche. He held the Hawken close to his chest, not that he thought he would have to use it. But a man in his friend's condition was too unpredictable to say for sure.

Loose dirt and small stones spewed out from under the driving hooves of Sawyer's mount. The animal was on its last legs and slipped several times. Jeremiah pounded it furiously with his fist and rifle.

It added fuel to Nate's anger. He didn't believe in mistreating animals and he had never looked kindly on those who did. Some trappers stuck to the philosophy that the only way to master a horse was to beat the animal into submission, but Nate believed that a little kindness went a long way toward accomplishing the same goal.

The black stallion took the grade on the fly. Nate knew that in less than a minute he would catch his quarry. He saw Sawyer's mount stumble, drop to a knee, then rise again. The animal plodded instead of trotted; its head hung low.

Jeremiah Sawyer looked over his shoulder, cursed, and jumped to the ground. He ran toward the top of the grade, his moccasins raising tiny puffs of dust.

Nate didn't bother with the packhorse for the moment. He galloped on past, leaning low, the Hawken clutched in both hands. The summit of the grade was mere yards away when he pulled abreast of Sawyer. "Stop," he said.

A maniacal gleam lighting his features, Jeremiah slowed and swung his rifle, trying to knock Nate off the stallion. Nate had anticipated the swing and evaded it. Then, lashing out with the Hawken, he hit Jeremiah across the shoulders. Jeremiah landed in the dirt, face first.

Nate was off the stallion before Sawyer could rise. He tore the rifle from Jeremiah's grasp and trained his own on the man's chest. Jeremiah froze in the act of pushing to his feet, his face that of a beast at bay.

"Damn you, Nate! You had no right to stop me!"

"I had every right," Nate said, backing up a few strides so he would have room to maneuver if his friend came at him. "The state you're in, Lassiter is liable to kill you before you kill him. And I don't want Lassiter to know anyone is on his trail until we're ready to make our move. That way he won't be on his guard."

"Even if he did put windows in my skull, there's no way he'd know about you and Old Bill," Jeremiah said, rising slowly. He looked at the stallion. "Let me take your horse and go on by myself."

"No."

"Please," Jeremiah said. "For the sake of our friendship, you have to."

"It's because we're friends that I'm not about to let you go riding off half-cocked. Yellow Flower wouldn't want you to throw your life away on her account."

Jeremiah turned red, clenched his knobby fists, and took a menacing step. "How would you know what she'd want? She was my wife, not yours!"

"I knew here fairly well," Nate said calmly. "Well enough to know that she was a lot like Winona. She was as kind as the day is long, and as smart as can be." He noticed that the stallion had stopped shy of the summit and backed toward it. "Yes, she'd want you to avenge her, but she'd never stand still for your committing suicide. And that's exactly what you aim to do."

"You think you know everything," Jeremiah said bitterly, his tone that of a small child caught with his hand in the cookie jar.

"I wasn't born yesterday," Nate said.

The stallion turned as he came up and stood meekly while he grabbed the reins. Jeremiah made no move to interfere. Nate was so close to the top that he only needed to take a few steps to see over it, and curiosity got the better of him. Keeping one eye on the melancholy avenger, he sidled high enough to view the vista beyond.

A wide green valley bisected the trail, running north to south. A river, in turn, bisected the valley. Along its banks grew trees as well as patches of heavy brush. There was no sign of a fire or movement and Nate was about to climb on the stallion when he lowered his gaze to the opposite slope.

Someone was jogging up it toward him. As yet the figure was several hundred yards away, too far for Nate to note much other than it was an Indian. Ducking low, hoping he hadn't been spotted, Nate hastened toward Sawyer.

"Mount up. Quickly."

"What's wrong?" Jeremiah asked, having the presence of mind to obey.

"I think it's that Blood you were telling me

about. He's coming this way."

Jeremiah stopped. Lips quivering, the veins on his temples bulging, he had the look of a bear hound about to bolt after a griz. "Does he know we're here?"

"I can't see how," Nate said. He wagged the Hawken. "Do as I told you. We can't shoot him yet. His friends must be nearby, and they'd hear."

"So what?" Jeremiah said. "I say we end it now."

"It's not open to parley." Nate stepped into the stirrups. To the north stretched a grass covered tract bounded by a low spine. To the south reared a series of small bluffs interspersed with boulders and gullies. When Sawyer had complied, he motioned southward and let the tired pack animal go first.

The arid ground became rocky. Their horses left few tracks. Nate wanted to cover the impressions with handfuls of dirt, but there was no time. Into the nearest gully he went, there to dismount and creep back to the rim. They had sought cover none too soon.

A lithe form stood atop the grade. The warrior looked both ways, then down at his feet. He must have seen Nate's tracks because he promptly crouched and pressed his rifle to his shoulder.

"That's the Blood," Jeremiah whispered at Nate's elbow, his voice full of raw emotion.

Nate looked to see if the other man would do anything rash. Jeremiah had dug the fingers of both hands into the earth and was trembling uncontrollably. "Be patient," Nate coaxed. "Your time will come."

The Blood was studying their tracks. Apparently the prints confused him because he walked around and around the spot where they had clashed.

"He'll find us. I know he will," Jeremiah whispered.

Nate wasn't so certain. Indians differed in ability, just like whites. Some were excellent rifle shots, while some couldn't hit the broad side of a mountain with a cannon. Some, like the Comanches, were natural-born horsemen. Others, like the Blackfeet, only rode when they had to. And in any given tribe, only a handful qualified as outstanding trackers. The rest were no better or worse than the average mountain man.

This one appeared stumped. The Blood strode to the summit again, then back along the line of tracks to where Jeremiah had been knocked down. He scratched his chin, squatted, and shook his head. After a while he made an impatient gesture and jogged on eastward.

"Damn it all," Jeremiah said. "I wanted to make maggot food of the son of a bitch."

"We will when the time is ripe," Nate said, marking the Blood's progress. The warrior never looked back and eventually his silhouette dwindled to a black speck.

Sighing, Nate shifted on his heel to descend. Belatedly, he saw the flick of Sawyer's hands. A spray of dirt struck him flush in both eyes. Involuntarily, he blinked, and it felt as if he had just submerged his head in sand. Tears gushed, blurring his vision. He knew what was coming and tried to leap to one side.

A granite blow landed on Nate's head above

the right ear, and it was as if a bolt of weakness shot through him. His legs buckled of their own accord. He felt another jarring jolt when his head hit the ground. The world had gone black but he was still vaguely conscious, still aware of who he was and where he was. But even that was denied him moments later when another blow hurtled him into oblivion.

Jeremiah Sawyer raised the big rock a third time, then paused. There was a nasty gash in King's head, covered with trickling blood. Another swing might well kill him.

As much as Jeremiah craved revenge on those who had slain his family, he wasn't about to rub out one of his few friends to achieve it. He slowly lowered the bloody rock, took a deep breath to regain his self-control, and cast it aside.

"I'm sorry," Jeremiah said softly. "But I can't rest until the butchers have gone under." He reclaimed his rifle and slipped King's pistols under his own belt. Nate groaned, but made no move to resist.

The black stallion lifted its head as Jeremiah dashed toward it and grabbed for the reins. To his annoyance, the horse pranced backward, out of reach.

"Hold still, damn you," Jeremiah said. Taking a few steps, he lunged. His reflexes were no match for the stallion's, which skipped off, tossing its mane.

Unwilling to waste time chasing the animal down, Jeremiah climbed onto the horse he had been using and rode to the grade. The brief rest had given his mount a chance to catch its wind. It balked a little when he made for the top, but settled down after a sharp kick in the ribs.

Jeremiah rose in the saddle and stared eastward. He couldn't be positive if it was his imagination or not, but he swore that he saw the Blood far, far off, staring back at him. The image vanished when he blinked. Shrugging, he rode on down into the valley. The Blood could wait. First he wanted Lassiter.

The trees were deathly silent when Jeremiah rode up. It was a warning that all was not as it should be. Any prudent mountain man would have proceeded with caution. But Jeremiah rode boldly into the woods. He didn't care if the cutthroats saw him coming. They were going to pay, come hell or high water.

In due course Jeremiah reached the low bank of the shallow river. Rather than seek a spot to ford, he crossed right there. Or rather, he tried to, for no sooner had the horse stepped into the water than it gave out with a loud whinny and commenced struggling to pull its hooves free.

Jeremiah prodded the animal again and again. It tried valiantly to extract itself from the mud bog, without success.

"Come on, you mangy cayuse!" Jeremiah said. "You picked a pitiful time to give out on me."

The animal's legs made great sucking noises as it lifted first one, then the other. Try as it might, it was unable to raise a single limb clear of the mud. Jeremiah was left with no recourse other than to slide off and gingerly pick his way to the bank. He sank with every stride, but not as deep as the horse.

Jeremiah could ill afford to lose his mount. He studied the problem a bit and had decided to simply grip its reins and try to pull it out, when to his ears came the creak of leather accompanied by a low nicker.

Spinning, Jeremiah dashed under cover. As he flattened he saw two riders materialize on the other bank. One was the giant known as Bear. The other was the smallest of the butchers, whose name Jeremiah didn't know.

"I told you that I heard something," the small man said.

"And you were right," Bear said, surveying the vegetation. "But where's the owner?"

"Maybe it belonged to some pilgrim and strayed off," the small man said. "Go fetch Earl while I take a gander."

"Keep your eyes skinned, Snip." The giant nodded and trotted off.

Jeremiah was almost beside himself with glee. He'd caught the killers at long last. It would have been child's play to drop the one called Snip at that range, but Jeremiah held his fire. He was after bigger game.

Snip rode a dozen yards to the south and crossed. A gravel bar provided a natural bridge across the bog. His beady eyes swept the tree line the whole time, and he kept one finger on the trigger of his rifle.

Once on the near shore, Snip drew as close to the stuck horse as he could without endangering his own. He whistled to it, trying to lure it to the bank, but the hapless pack animal had sunk to the points of its hocks and could do no more than whinny helplessly.

Jeremiah was impatient for Lassiter and the rest to appear. He extended the rifle and sighted down the barrel at the same spot where the two cutthroats had appeared. Listen as he might, he heard nothing.

"I wish I had me a rope," Snip was saying. "I'd have you out of there."

Dismounting, Snip walked to the edge of the bog and leaned forward as far as he dared. His fingers brushed the animal's tail. "There has to be a way," he said to himself.

Fifteen feet away, Jeremiah scarcely breathed. He probed the stretch of river for evidence of Lassiter, his body tingling with excitement. Snip hardly interested him. He paid scant attention when the killer paced back and forth as if mulling over how best to free the horse. He didn't give Snip a second look when the man walked to his mount and fiddled with a saddlebag. But he did go as rigid as a plank when Snip suddenly looked in his direction.

The cutthroat wore a mocking sort of smile, as if gloating. It made no sense to Jeremiah until, with a start, he realized that Snip was looking at something behind him. At the same instant he heard a soft scraping noise, as of a bush rubbing buckskin.

Jeremiah knew that if he twisted, Snip would see him. Yet a terrible feeling came over him that, if he didn't turn, he would regret it. For a few moments he wavered.

Suddenly a pair of steely hands swooped down, one closing on the rifle, the other on the back of Jeremiah's neck. He was wrenched into the air and shaken as a terrier might shake a rabbit. And then he found himself staring up into the twisted visage of the huge killer called Bear.

Chapter Nine

Nate King and Jeremiah Sawyer were barely out of sight when Old Bill Zeigler smiled and turned to Winona and the children.

"What has you so happy?" Zachary asked while trying to catch a last glimpse of his pa.

"Life, boy," Bill said. "If you were to live long enough, you'd find that life has a sense of humor all its own. From the cradle to the grave, life is one big laugh."

"I don't think I agree," Zach said.

"Ask me if I care?" Old Bill said, and with deceptive speed he hauled off and rammed the stock of his rifle into the youngster's side, which sent Zach tumbling from the saddle, doubled over in agony.

Winona was so shocked that she sat as one transformed to stone for the few moments it took Old Bill to swing the muzzle of his rifle around to cover her.

"I wouldn't lift a finger against me, were I you," the mountain man said. "Not if you're partial to breathing." He snatched her rifle and threw it down, then stripped her of her pistol and knife. She offered no resistance, which would have been hard to do in any case, with Evelyn in her arms.

"There, now!" Old Bill said, grinning. He moved his mount a few yards away so he could keep track of all three of them. "At long last my patience has been rewarded."

Bewildered beyond measure, Winona saw her son roll from side to side, sputtering through clenched teeth. She wanted to go to him, but was leery of the possible consequences. "We thought you were our friend!" she said.

"Your mistake, not mine," Zeigler said gruffly. "I can't help it if I'm so darned good at actin' that I can fool most any man alive, white or red."

"The whole time you have been pretending to like us?"

"Playing you all for jackasses," Old Bill said. "All these days I've been bidin' my time, waitin' for the opportunity I was sure would come. And it did."

"But why?" Winona asked. It staggered her that she had let herself be duped, that she had been taken in by a man whose nature was akin to that of the killers they chased.

Long ago, as a young woman, Winona had learned that some whites were deceitful, that they secretly harbored strong lusts and perverse longings. Once, when her family had attended a rendezvous, a white man had entered their lodge without permission and tried to have his way with her. Only the timely intervention of her father had stopped him.

The experience had taught Winona to always be on the lookout for such men and to avoid them as if they had the pox. Since marrying Nate, she had rarely been bothered, and as a result she had let down her guard when she shouldn't have. There was really only one man any woman could trust fully and completely, and that was her husband.

"We'll chaw later, woman," Old Bill said. "For now, we have to put a lot of miles behind us before your man comes back. Soon as your boy quits his bellyachin', we'll be on our way, pack animals and all."

Unknown to Zeigler, Zachary King's pain had subsided. He was sore but otherwise unharmed, and he wanted nothing more than to draw his pistol and put a ball through the man's skull. The only thing that stopped him was the rifle Zeigler held on his mother. All it would take was a twitch of a finger as Zeigler fell, and his mother or his sister might pay with their lives for his brash action.

Old Bill glanced down. "I reckon you've moaned and groaned long enough, boy. Why, when I was your age, a little tap like I gave you wouldn't have made me blink. On your feet now and keep your hands where I can see them."

It was the very last thing Zach wanted to do, yet he felt he had no choice. He uncoiled and stood, poised to draw if the mountain man lowered his guard. But Old Bill held that rifle steady on his mother's chest.

"Drop the flintlock and your knife. Then climb on your paint."

Once again Zach complied. His mother gave him a sympathetic look that only made him feel worse. With his pa gone, it was his responsibility to protect the women in their family. And he had failed.

Winona dearly desired to spare her children, so she said, "I am the one you want. Leave Zach and Evelyn here. They pose no danger to you."

"Goodness, you think right highly of yourself," Old Bill said. "I couldn't give an owl's ass about you, Shoshone. You're involved because I can't leave any witnesses."

Confused, Winona said, "But if not for me, then why?"

Old Bill grinned at her son. "For him. Now move out before I take it into my head to shoot the girl."

Both mother and son were confounded by the revelation. Paralyzing fear seized Winona, and she meekly goaded her mare into motion.

Zachary was flabbergasted. He couldn't understand why the old man was going to slay them on his account. "What did I ever do to you?" he asked.

"You hit me, boy."

"That time I walloped you with the rifle when you were fixing to stab my pa?"

"Know of any other time?" Old Bill said brusquely. "That once was enough. I made up my mind then and there that I'd fix you and fix you proper for the hurt you caused me." His voice lowered to a growl. "No one lays a hand on William T. Zeigler and lives to tell of it. No one."

"But he's just a boy!" Winona said, disbelief and fury vying for dominance in her heart. "He was doing what any other boy would do."

"Maybe so," Old Bill said. "And I'd do the same to any other boy."

Winona had known whites to do things that were judged extremely peculiar by the standards of her people, but this, as her husband would say, beat them all. What sort of man would hold a noble act against someone of her son's tender years? Perhaps the horrible tales told about Old Bill stemmed from a kernel of truth. The somber thought prompted her to ask, "Do you eat people? Is that what this is all about?"

Zeigler's eyes twinkled. "Heard that one, have you? I suppose pretty near everyone in the Rockies has."

"Do you?" Winona said.

"I'm not sayin' I do. I'm not sayin' I don't," Old Bill said. "Let's keep it as a surprise for later, after we get to where we're going."

"Where would that be?" Zach asked.

"All in good time, boy," Old Bill said. "All in good time."

Zach saw his mother clutch Evelyn to her and felt a strange lump form in his throat. He gave the lead rope a sharp tug to move the packhorses along. Then he said, "You made a big mistake, mister. My pa will be after us before too long. And I wouldn't want to be in your moccasins when he gets his hands on you."

"Spare me the bluster, brat," Zeigler said. "Your father might be fringed hell on two legs, but I'm no slouch myself. I always stay two steps ahead of everyone else by thinkin' ahead. This time will be no different. I have a little surprise in store for your pa that will put an end to the high and mighty Grizzly Killer forever."

Zachary became so mad, his temples throbbed. He recollected all the times his pa had warned him about being too trusting for his own good. "Trust has to be earned", his father often said. To take it for granted that someone was dependable was a sure way of inviting trouble.

Yet Zach had done just that. Old Bill had seemed so friendly, even after being konked on the noggin, that Zach had assumed that the old-timer was a harmless coot. He wondered if his pa had also been deceived, and he figured that had to be the case or his father wouldn't have gone off and left them alone with Zeigler—unless his pa had counted on him to protect his mother and sister.

Depressed, Zach glared at the mountain man and noticed Old Bill staring off at a flock of sparrows winging eastward. "You can see just as well as we can!"

"Of course I can," Old Bill said. "Fact is, I can probably see better than the lot of you. My eyes have always been as sharp as an eagle's."

Zach was quick to discern something else. "You lied to my pa. You attacked him on purpose."

"Sure did. I was hoping to slit his throat and take his rifle from him before your ma or you could interfere, but he was too damned fast for me."

"It isn't right, what you do," Zach said resentfully. "It isn't right to go around hurting others for no reason."

"Oh, I've got me a dandy reason," Old Bill said,

and he smacked his lips loudly a few times.

"You're vermin, mister, plain and simple."

Old Bill's lips compressed into a tight line. "That's enough out of you, pup. I want you to quit your jawing. I won't stand for being pestered. Just ride along as if you're out on a Sunday jaunt and we'll get along right fine."

Young Zachary King did as he was told, but inwardly he seethed like a boiling volcano. He was not going to let Zeigler harm his father or mother or sister. Somehow, he would turn the tables on their captor.

Brule rarely smiled. It wasn't in his nature to find much amusement in life. But outwitting others always made him feel good. Which was why he smiled broadly now as he trotted eastward along the same rutted track he had been following in the opposite direction for so long.

The warrior had grown tired of the company of whites. Their mindless chatter, their constant bickering, their body odor—all had made him long for the companionship of his own kind. And since that was denied him, he preferred to be by himself.

Brule hadn't bothered to inform Earl Lassiter and the others. That morning Lassiter had sent him off to spy on the whites in the wagons, as usual. Only this time Brule had merely gone a short distance and then circled around to the east. Lassiter and the rest were probably still waiting for him to return and report.

Brule slowed down to study his trail. There was no sign of pursuit, nor did he truly think

Lassiter would be stupid enough to send someone to bring him back.

Brule gave his splendid new knife a pat, then admired his new rifle. As distasteful as it had been to associate with whites, he had to admit that he had benefited greatly. Perhaps he would do it again one day.

Running on, Brule settled into a steady stride. He thought of the tracks he had seen at the grade and of the two whites who had watched him from the gully without being aware that he knew they were there. Who had they been? Why had they fought? Even more perplexing, why had they hid from him instead of ambushing him when he came over the summit?

Brule had no burning interest to learn the answers. If the pair were after Lassiter, it was Lassiter's problem. He wanted nothing more to do with the renegades.

Then the Blood came to where a number of riders and packhorses had come on the wagon trail from the south. He studied the many tracks closely, reading them as a white would read a book. He saw where two men had ridden westward and one had returned. He was able to tell that another man had then gone after the first. They were the pair at the grade, he realized.

Five horses had gone south again. Brule guessed that two of them were heavily burdened pack animals. The third horse carried lighter weight, perhaps a child or a small man or woman. The fourth horse, which was shod, carried a full-grown man. And the last animal, if the depth of the mare's tracks were any indication, was being ridden by a woman. Since this horse wasn't shod, Brule suspected the woman to be an Indian, which changed everything.

Brule had not been with a female in many sleeps. White women revolted him; they were puny, pale whiners, about as attractive as slugs. He did not know of a single warrior of any tribe who had taken a white woman as a wife because they were so widely regarded as unable to adapt to the Indian way of life.

Lassiter had surprised Brule by telling him that white women felt the same way about Indian men. In Brule's estimation it was typical of white women that they were too stupid to appreciate worthy mates. He, for instance, was a skilled fighter and hunter. If he had a wife, she would never want for meat or hides. And the many coup he earned would bring honor to their lodge. Any woman in her right mind would leap at the chance to be his mate.

Brule straightened and scowled. He must not think about such things. Being an outcast, he would never know the joy of having a Blood wife, never rise in standing in his tribe to one day be a war chief as he had always dreamed of doing.

But just because a Blood wife was denied him did not necessarily mean Brule couldn't have another. Any Indian woman would do. And here was one ripe for the taking.

Brule gazed eastward. It had been in his head to travel to the prairie, but another idea appealed to him. Swinging to the south, he trotted on the trail of the three riders.

A cool breeze on his face was the first sensation Nate King felt upon reviving. He lay still a few moments, his head racked by drumming pangs, trying to remember what had happened. When he did, he shot up into a sitting position and winced as the torment worsened. Blinking, he looked around.

The sun crowned the western horizon. Soon twilight would descend. Jeremiah Sawyer was gone. The black stallion stood 50 feet off, nibbling at a small patch of brown grass.

Nate carefully ran his fingers over his wound. A coat of slick dry blood matted his hair and clung to his ear, cheek, and neck. He rubbed his cheek but the blood wouldn't come off. Retrieving his hat and Hawken, he slowly stood, and in doing so he discovered that both of his pistols were missing.

The stallion saw him shuffling forward and walked over to meet him. Nate leaned against the big black for support, stroking its neck. "Good boy," he said softly.

Nate donned the hat, gripped the saddle, and pulled himself up. For a few moments the landscape seemed to dance as if alive, and he thought he would lose his hold and fall. Forking a leg, he slumped down on the stallion's neck and breathed deeply while regaining his strength.

At length Nate straightened and rode up out of the gully. At the Oregon Trail, he drew rein. From the tracks it was clear that Jeremiah had gone into the valley. Nate had to make up his mind whether to go after him or to rejoin his family.

Nate told himself that he was under no personal obligation. Jeremiah had been a friend, but that had been a totally different Jeremiah Sawyer, a man very much like Nate, a fellow free trapper who had taken an Indian wife and become a devoted husband and father. Unlike the majority of trappers, who took wives for a single season and then cast them aside or merely indulged when they could pay the price, the two of them always regarded their marriages as seriously as they would if they were wed to white women. It was no wonder they had become close friends, they were so much alike.

But as far as Nate was concerned, Jeremiah had severed the ties that bound them by trying to beat in his head with a rock. He shouldn't bother trying to save Jeremiah from himself. The man had made his choice and had to live with it.

Nate lifted the reins and went to head eastward. To his mind's eye appeared an image from the last rendezvous, when the two families had sat around a fire late at night swapping tales and joking. He remembered Jeremiah passing a whiskey jug to him after taking a long swig, and how they had both laughed when little Evelyn got a hold of Winona's nose and wouldn't let go.

"Damn it all," Nate muttered, turning the stallion. He went over the summit at a gallop, no longer caring about stealth. He couldn't just ride off and leave Jeremiah to face the killers alone, no matter what had happened.

Nate was grateful that Winona and the children were safe. Should anything befall him, Bill Zeigler was on hand to help Winona reach their cabin. He could rest easy and concentrate on the renegades.

Suddenly Nate spied several large black birds wheeling high in the sky above the river. "Buzzards," he said aloud and rode faster until the cottonwoods closed around him. Here he halted and secured the reins to a low limb.

Never take anything for granted—that was the creed Nate lived by, and he applied it by crawling through the undergrowth to a vantage point that afforded an unobstructed view of the river. He could see the vultures, seven in all, swooping steadily lower. Toward what? he wondered, then saw a bulky form lying at the water's edge. It was too big to be a man.

Nate bided his time. Several buzzards landed, one on top of the carcass. Its hooked beak tore into the hide as neatly as a knife, ripping an opening so the scavenger could get at the juicy flesh underneath. Strips of red meat were ripped off and greedily gulped.

Nothing else moved along the river. Nate searched the shadows long and hard. He wouldn't put it past Lassiter to try to lure him into a trap, but after ten minutes he grew convinced the coast was clear.

Still, to be safe, Nate hugged the ground as he snaked close enough to identify the carcass. He believed it was a horse, but he had no idea it would turn out to be the packhorse, partially buried in mud. Someone had slit the animal's throat and left it to meet a slow, grisly end, its lifeblood pumping into the bog in which it had been stuck.

Rising, Nate stalked as close as he could without sinking. There was no trace of Jeremiah. And with the sun gone, it would soon be too dark to track. He decided to try anyway, since his friend's life was at stake, and he turned to hurry to the stallion.

A guttural groan fluttered on the wind, arising somewhere to the north of where Nate stood. He walked toward the source, scouring the brush at ground level. Under a massive willow, he stopped to listen. Time passed and the groan was repeated. Only it came from above.

Nate tilted his head back and gasped. He had witnessed many gruesome atrocities since taking up residence in the untamed Rockies, but few equaled the ghastly savagery Jeremiah Sawyer had suffered.

The renegades had stripped him and peeled his skin from his body as if he were an orange. His fingers and toes had been hacked off, his ears smashed to a pulp, his nose sliced down the middle. Then they had tied a rope to his wrists and hauled him ten feet off the ground. As if that wasn't enough, someone on horseback had thrust a knife into his gut and left the knife there. A loathsome pool of blood had formed under the doomed man.

Quickly Nate scrambled into the tree. Working from branch to branch, he reached the limb to which Jeremiah was tied. He hesitated before applying his knife, then did. He tried to catch the rope before Jeremiah fell. The weight was too much for him, the rope searing his palms so badly he had to let go or lose all his skin. He winced when his friend smacked wetly into the pool.

Clambering swiftly down, Nate dashed over and knelt. Jeremiah's good eye closed and he was breathing heavily. Nate touched his head and almost jumped back when Jeremiah's lid snapped wide open.

"Nate?" The word was croaked, Jeremiah's pupil dilated and unfocused.

"I'm right here," Nate said, reaching for a hand that wasn't there. He didn't know what else to do so he put both his hands on Jeremiah's head.

"You were right all the time. I should have listened." Jeremiah licked red froth from his lips. "The Blood ran off on them. They were hunting for him when they saw me. Tricked me, the bastards. Made me think one of them was going back for the rest when all the time he was circling around behind me."

"Don't talk," Nate said when his friend took a breath. "You should lie quietly."

"For how long?" Jeremiah said weakly. "You have no idea of the pain. It's worse than I can describe."

Nate swallowed his building grief and said, "I wish there was something I could do."

"There is."

"What?"

"Kill me."

"No," Nate said.

"You have to. I hurt so bad. Please."

"No."

"You know I'll die anyway," Jeremiah said, tears streaming from the corners of his eyes. "Don't let me suffer. Deprive them of that, at least."

"I—" Nate said, but couldn't finish. He knew what he had to do but he couldn't bring himself to accept it.

"I'm waiting," Jeremiah said forlornly.

Nate lowered his leaden right hand to his butcher knife, then froze. The thought of burying the blade in his friend's ribs was one he couldn't abide. He didn't care how close the renegades were. He picked up the Hawken and thumbed back the hammer. As Nate lightly pressed the muzzle to the other man's temple, Jeremiah twisted his neck.

"I don't blame you, pard. You did all you could." Jeremiah coughed. "Just do me one favor."

"Anything."

"Make them pay."

"You have my word," Nate King said huskily, then stroked the trigger.

Chapter Ten

Katie Brandt was in the process of making a pot of fresh coffee when a shot echoed across the darkening valley. She glanced anxiously up at her husband, who was mending harness while seated on the tongue of their wagon. "Was that a shot?"

"It was," Glen said, standing. Against the wagon leaned his rifle, which he picked up.

"But who could be shooting? We're all here."

That they were, the Ringcrest family across the clearing by their wagon, the Potter clan at ease on a blanket spread out on the soft grass.

"Your guess is as good as mine," Glen said.

"Do you think it might be hostiles?"

"Mighty careless hostiles, if it is," Glen said. "Indians don't like to advertise their presence. It could be a trapper shooting his supper. I doubt he has any notion we're here."

Katie stood, flashing her teeth in joy. "Do you

really think so? Oh, I do so hope you're right! It's been ages since we talked to anyone besides our companions. Wouldn't it be nice to have a guest in camp? Maybe you should go see."

The idea disturbed Glen. It was bad enough that they had been stuck in a small clearing on the west side of an unnamed valley for over a day while repairing Peter Ringcrest's broken wheel. Hemmed in by trees, they were sitting ducks for savages inclined to deprive them of their lives or their belongings or both.

Six days had gone by since Katie had seen the Indian. So far they had seen neither hide nor hair of any hostiles. The others were of the opinion that they had been needlessly worried, but Glen didn't share their outlook. He had a nagging feeling that they were all in grave peril. And if his hunch was right, it would be stupid of him to go off alone.

At the same time, Glen had no desire to appear yellow in front of his new bride. So when no one objected to her proposal, he started for the ring of vegetation.

"Hold on," Bob Potter said. Like Glen, he had grabbed his rifle and stood peering into the woods. "Maybe you should wait until we know who is out there."

"We'll never know who it is if one of us doesn't look," Peter Ringcrest said. "And we'd better do it before it's too dark to be abroad."

"I'll go," Glen said, secretly hoping someone would stop him. No one did though, so he squared his shoulders and strode into the trees. Thanks to the glow cast by the trio of cooking fires, the area was lit up as bright as day for all of five paces.

Then the darkness closed in like a murky veil and he could hardly see his hand in front of his face.

Glen was surprised that Katie had suggested he go. Usually she couldn't bear to have him stray out of her sight. He knew she had been embarrassed by her show of fear at the spring and further embarrassed when hostiles failed to materialize. Just the night before she had confided that she was beginning to think it had been a friendly Indian she scared off by acting like a ten year old.

Was she trying to prove she could cope when alone by having him search for the shooter? Glen didn't know, but it was the only logical explanation. Then again, as he'd learned during the short time he'd been married, trying to figure women out was guaranteed to give a man a headache.

Glen halted and listened. The shot had come from the vicinity of the river but he heard no other sounds from that direction. Being by himself in the dark brought gooseflesh to his skin. Steadying his nerves, he slowly advanced.

Seconds passed, and Glen thought he saw something move off to the right. Leveling the rifle, he said quietly, "Who's there?"

No one replied.

Chalking it up to his imagination, Glen went on. He held the rifle tucked tightly to his side, ready to fire at the vaguest hint of a threat to his life. Every few steps he stopped to look around. His skin crawled as if covered with thousands of bugs and his hands became clammy with sweat.

Glen covered 50 or 60 feet, then stopped. There was no need for him to go the whole mile and a half. None of the others would ever know if he simply waited a suitable interval and then returned to inform them he had not seen anyone. What harm could it do? he asked himself.

Five minutes went by. Glen began to feel guilty. He had told his wife he would go see, and here he was cowering among the cottonwoods. What sort of husband would deceive his wife? What kind of man had he become if he was so willing to lie to his friends?

Glen hiked deeper into the trees. An owl hooted to the south and was answered by another to the north. Yet another hooted to his rear.

That was strange, Glen reflected. He'd seldom heard so many owls sound off at the same time. It brought to mind stories he had been told about the uncanny ability of Indians to mimic animal cries. Turning, he sought some sign of the nocturnal birds of prey.

Above him, something rustled. Glen heard a creak and looked up in time to see a vague form swooping down on him from a branch. He tried to bring the rifle up but the form slammed into him before he could. The breath whooshed from his lungs as he crashed onto his back with a heavy weight astride his chest.

Glen was aware he had lost his rifle. He attempted to lift his arms but a knee kicked him in the gut, rendering him as weak as a kitten. Footsteps converged and his arms were seized. It all happened so fast that he was being held upright between two men in buckskins before he quite collected his wits.

"Well, what have we here?" said a tall specimen with a face as hard as iron. "You should have stayed in the States, pilgrim. The climate out here isn't good for your health."

Others laughed, and Glen realized there were five men, all told. "Who are you men? What do you want?" he demanded. He assumed they were trappers who had mistaken him for a prowling Indian and would release him at any moment.

The tall man tapped Glen's head. "Not too bright, this one." He poked Glen in the chest. "The name is Lassiter. I've seen you before. We've been following your little caravan for a while now."

"Why didn't you show yourselves?" Glen said. "We wouldn't shoot at white men. I'm Glen Brandt, and you can take my word for it that all of you would have been welcome to enter our camp at any time."

A tall man laughed. "Now ain't you just about the friendliest idiot I've ever run into!"

"Idiot?" Glen said.

Lassiter shot Bear a sharp glance, then put on his best smile and gave the young man a friendly pat on the shoulder. "Don't mind him. He's been hit once too many times on the head. His thinker is puny." Gesturing for Dixon and Kingslow to let Brandt go, he said, "I'm sorry for the rough treatment. We didn't know if you were friendly or not, and a body can't be any too careful in the wild."

"Believe me, I know," Glen said, happy the mistake had been remedied. He rubbed his sore stomach. "It's my fault. I shouldn't have been creeping about in the dark, but we've been afraid of tangling with hostiles ever since my wife spotted a savage."

"Hostiles, you say?" Lassiter said. "If that's the case, maybe we should join forces. We're heading west too. With us along, you'd be better able to protect your womenfolk."

"There's an idea!" Glen said. With five more rifles to rely on, his party could drive off any number of hostiles.

Because of the darkness, the young farmer couldn't see the sly grins that nipped at the mouth of every man there except the giant. Bear was befuddled by the talk of joining the pilgrims on their trek. After days and days of considering how best to wipe the pilgrims out, it was incomprehensible to him that Lassiter was acting so friendly.

"I don't get it," Bear said. "I thought you told us—"

Lassiter knew Bear well enough to foresee his blunder. Giving Bear a playful but hard elbow jab in the ribs, he forced a laugh and said, "Yes, I told you that we should swing on around the caravan and go on by ourselves, but I've changed my mind."

"Oh," Bear said dully, still at a loss to understand. But the cold look Lassiter gave him kept him from opening his mouth again.

Glen Brandt had paid no attention to the exchange. He had walked over to his rifle and picked it up. Delighted by his stroke of good fortune, he clapped Lassiter on the back and said, "Follow me. I'll hail the camp so they don't open fire."

"We'd be obliged," Lassiter said. He cannily waited until the young innocent had taken a few strides, then said, "Hold on just a second. I have to send someone for our horses."

Gesturing for his men to gather close, Lassiter

whispered, "Bear, you fetch the animals and keep your mouth shut. I don't want you spoiling things."

"What about that shot we heard?" Dixon asked.

Snip stared toward the river. "That's right. It must be a friend of that guy we strung up."

"We'll worry about it later," Lassiter said. "Right now the pilgrims are all that matter. Keep your fingers on your triggers and be ready to follow my lead."

Glen had stopped to wait for them. He wondered why they saw fit to speak so quietly. "Is everything all right? You're not changing your minds, are you?"

Lassiter faced him, smiling. "Not on your life. Lead the way. We'll be right behind you."

It never failed to amaze Lassiter how gullible some folks could be. They were too damned trusting for their own good. They assumed everyone was as meek as they were, when anyone with half a brain knew that it was a dog-eat-dog world, every man for himself. The survivors were those who trusted no one, who preyed on weak fools like Brandt just as wolves preyed on flocks of sheep.

Lassiter was in such good humor that he whistled to himself as he strolled in the wake of the pilgrim. At the back of his mind was a speck of unease over the shot they had heard, but he put it from his thoughts for the time being. They would deal with whoever was out there just as they had dealt with Jeremiah Sawyer.

Presently fires flared in the night. Lassiter saw figures moving about, men, women, and children. The sight of the women made his mouth water.

Glen waved an arm and shouted, "I'm coming

in! And I'm bringing friends! Whatever you do, don't shoot!"

In the clearing, Katie Brandt saw the startled looks on the others. They were thinking the same thing she was—it might be a trick of some kind. Peter Ringcrest and Bob Potter moved closer to the edge of the clearing, their rifles at the ready. Katie joined the women and children at the Potter wagon. The girls hid behind their mother's skirt while little Charley Potter had found a stick which he held as if it were a club.

Then Glen appeared, grinning happily. "We won't have to worry about hostiles any more," he said. "I've met some trappers."

Katie's heart leaped into her throat at the sight of their saviors. They were as cruel looking a bunch as she had ever set eyes on. The tallest, in particular, gave her the same gaze she might give a haunch of beef she was fixing to buy. It sent a shiver down her spine.

"This here is Lassiter," Glen said. "There's one more but he went to get their horses."

Lassiter offered his hand to the men. He listened with half an ear as they told him their names, his eyes lingering on the three women. The youngest was a genuine beauty, a vision of loveliness made real. Often he had dreamed of women like her, but never in his wildest cravings had he ever expected to make love to one.

"I'm pleased to meet all of you," Lassiter said. He was also pleased to see Dixon, Kingslow, and Snip fanning casually out to either side. "Hope we didn't spook you folks none."

"Not at all," Peter Ringcrest said, setting the stock of his rifle on the ground. "As the Bible says, we must love our neighbors. Make yourselves comfortable. We have plenty of coffee to share."

Dixon looked expectantly at Lassiter but Lassiter gave a single shake of his head and moved over to a fire. Sitting cross-legged, he accepted a tin cup and grinned at the young woman, who came over to pour for him. "That's right nice of you, ma'am," he said.

"My pleasure," Katie said, although her insides were balled as tight as a fist. Her every instinct shrieked at her to get as far away from the newcomers as she could, but she dismissed the feeling as childish. The other four had also sat down and were being just as gracious as their leader.

Lassiter made a show of scanning the wagons and the livestock. "It's mighty brave of you to be heading for the Oregon Country with as small a party as you have," he said, then took a sip. The coffee had been sweetened with sugar, a rare treat. He figured there must be bags of the sweetener in the wagons, enough to last him a year. And who knew what else?

"Have you been there?" Peter Ringcrest asked.

"Can't say as I have," Lassiter said.

"Well, I have," Ringcrest said, "on the Lord's work. And I'm here to tell you that mortal man hasn't set eyes on prettier land anywhere. It's as if the Lord gave the land his personal blessing."

Lassiter arched an eyebrow. "From the way you talk, I gather you're a religious man."

"I'm a missionary," Ringcrest said stiffly. "Dr. Whitman and I are associates."

"Who?"

"Marcus Whitman. Surely you've heard of him?

He was quite the sensation at the rendezvous."

"Must have been a rendezvous I missed," Lassiter said. The fact was that he had heard of Whitman and the holier-than-thou types who were determined to convert the Indians whether the Indians wanted to be converted or not. Their gall put a bitter taste in Lassiter's mouth.

"We're the first of a wave of settlers who will stream to Oregon now that the way has been opened," Ringcrest said. "Dr. Whitman expects that within ten to fifteen years the territory will be able to apply for statehood."

"How nice," Lassiter said dryly.

"Maybe sooner, once all the tribes forsake their heathen ways and accept Christianity," Ringcrest said.

"Maybe you should keep in mind that a lot of mountain men share those heathen ways, as you call them," Lassiter said.

"To the ruin of their eternal souls. It behooves all of us to anchor ourselves in the Bible and not allow temptation to carry us adrift on the wayward seas of life."

Lassiter swallowed more coffee to relieve the bitter taste, then said, "Whatever you say, Parson." He could tell by the way some of his men were fidgeting that they were growing impatient, and he didn't blame them. But the young woman and Bob Potter still regarded them suspiciously and he wanted all of the pilgrims off their guard when he made his move. "Are all of you missionaries?" he asked.

"Goodness, no," Glen Brandt said. "I aim to be a farmer, and Bob is a tinker by trade. If your knives need sharpening, he's the man to see."

"Do tell?" Lassiter said, brightening as an idea occurred to him. Pulling out his butcher knife, he extended it, hilt first. "Then here you go, mister. I reckon all of us could use our blades honed." He glanced meaningfully at his men. "All of us."

Ben Kingslow was quickest to deduce Lassiter's motive. "Ain't that the truth," he said. "Here's my knife too. I want an edge sharp enough to split a hair."

In short order Bob Potter had all their knives. He acted bewildered by their request, as if it was the very last thing he had expected them to do. His wife held his rifle since he had his hands full. "Mark my words, gentleman," he said. "When I'm done, you'll be able to shave with these."

"Have at it," Lassiter said, and he had to down more coffee to keep from laughing when the pilgrim headed for his wagon. The young woman, Katie, was still watching them warily, so he said, "First you share your coffee. Now you take care of our knives. We'd like to show our appreciation by doing something for you."

"There's no need," Ringcrest said. "Sharing is reward in itself for those who walk in the steps of the Lord."

"There must be something we can do," Lassiter said. "If we're going to travel together, I insist on doing our part to help out. We can hunt and cook for you."

"You cook, Mr. Lassiter?" Katie asked skeptically.

"Sure, ma'am."

"Most men regard cooking as womens' work. They won't touch a pot or ladle with a ten-foot pole."

Lassiter could be a charmer when he wanted, and he was his most disarming when he said, "Heck, Mrs. Brandt. When a man lives by his lonesome in the mountains, he learns soon enough which end of a ladle is which." He was pleased when she grinned and turned away. At last the pilgrims were all convinced that he and his men were friendly. The fools.

"Matter of fact," Lassiter said, "tomorrow, for supper, we'll fix venison like you've never tasted before. You just leave the hunting, carving, and everything to us."

"Why, aren't you the perfect gentlemen?" Ringcrest's wife said.

"We try our best," Lassiter said. Lowering the cup, he held his right hand close to his thigh and wagged a finger at Dixon, who nodded and slowly stood. Kingslow shifted so he was facing Bob Potter. Snip swiveled so he could keep his eyes on Ringcrest, who was talking to his son.

It was a moment Lassiter savored. He was about to educate the unsuspecting pilgrims in one of the harsher realities of life, a lesson they would never forget during the short span allotted them on earth. It tickled him, having hoodwinked them the way he had. It confirmed his own opinion that he was smarter than most men.

Katie Brandt stepped to her husband and took his hand. As nice as the trappers were being, she couldn't shake a troubling feeling that all was not well. Looking at Lassiter made her uncomfortable, as if she were gazing at the visage of a mad dog about to pounce.

Glen grinned at her. He knew her well enough to sense that something was amiss, but not well enough yet to pinpoint the cause. Squeezing her hand, he said softly, "What has you worried? Everything will be all right now that these men are here to help us."

"I hope so," Katie said softly so only he would hear.

Lassiter saw them huddled together and casually draped a hand on his rifle, which lay propped against his leg. "Well, I guess now is as good a time as any."

"For what?" Peter Ringcrest asked.

"For this," Lassiter said and shot the missionary through the chest. He acted so swiftly that none of the pilgrims had time to react. Then Mrs. Ringcrest screamed and Potter's wife shrieked. Potter started toward him with a knife in hand, but drew up short when Ben Kingslow covered him. Young Glen Brandt went to lift his rifle, but froze when Dixon trained a muzzle on his wife. The children merely gawked, too stunned to think.

Lassiter rose and moved to the fallen man. Ringcrest still lived, his eyes wide in astonishment, his lips working feebly.

"Why? In God's name, man, why?"

"I wanted to," Lassiter said. He kicked the missionary in the mouth, then smirked when blood spurted out and Ringcrest writhed in agony. "You like to go around preaching love for all. Me, I like to go around doing as I damn well please. And it pleases me to take your life and everything else that belongs to you."

"You monster!" The howl of outrage came from little Charley Ringcrest, who launched himself at Lassiter with his stick upraised. Lassiter got his arm up to deflect the blow. Spinning, he backhanded the boy across the face. Charley fell onto his side, gritted his teeth in fury, and rose to attack again.

Snip shot the boy through the head at near point-blank range. The back of Charley's skull exploded outward, showering gore and brains all over Mrs. Ringcrest, who promptly fainted.

"Anyone else care to die?" Lassiter said, regarding each of the pilgrims in turn. "I'd rather keep you alive for a while, but I'm not going to force you to live longer if you don't want to."

"You bastard!" Glen Brandt growled.

In two strides Lassiter reached him and struck with all his might. His fist crunched into the younger man's cheek, splitting the flesh and flattening Brandt where he stood. Katie made a move to help, but Lassiter wagged a finger at her. "Don't even think it."

Katie blanched, scared to the core of her being, her wits scrambled by the terrible turn of events. "What do you want with us?"

"Why, I should think that would be obvious," Earl Lassiter said, reaching out to stroke her long golden hair. His sadistic laugh wavered on the night wind.

Chapter Eleven

Winona King kept hoping against hope that her demented captor would turn his back or otherwise give her an opening she could exploit, but the crafty mountain man never did.

Until half an hour before sunset they wound southward along the same route they had followed north. Zach and she were leading packhorses; Bill Zeigler was bringing up the rear, far enough back to drop either of them if they tried anything.

Zach was also alert for a chance to do something, although he had no idea what. Dashing off into the undergrowth would be pointless. He'd escape, but it would leave his mother and sister in Zeigler's clutches. He had to slay the man, a hopeless task without a weapon.

Old Bill reined up on the north side of a narrow creek. "This is far enough for today," he said. "I want both of you to climb down. And don't try anything. I know all the tricks there are. You'd only get yourselves killed."

Zachary eyed a parfleche draped behind his saddle as he dismounted. It contained, among other things, a small knife he used when whittling. Somehow he had to get his hands on it.

Zeigler had climbed down and moved to a convenient log. His rifle was pointed right at Winona. "Here's the way it will be. You'll fix supper, squaw. The brat will go gather wood for our fire. But first you put that cradleboard down over here by me. Keep in mind that if either one of you gets any contrary notions, I'll shoot the papoose. And don't think I won't."

Helplessness and frustration seared Winona like red-hot coals. She obeyed, giving her precious daughter a kiss as she straightened up. "If you harm her—"

"Oh, please," Zeigler said, cutting her off, "save your threats. You're in no position to do a damn thing, and you know it. And you don't want to get me riled."

Winona gazed toward the Oregon Trail. How long would it be, she wondered, before Nate showed up? Would he suspect what had happened? Or would he ride blindly into Zeigler's sights and be cut down before she could warn him?

"Get crackin' with them vittles, Shoshone," Old Bill said. "All this ridin' has given me a powerful appetite."

"What would you like?"

"We have some jerked deer meat left, as I recollect. Fix me a stew and throw in some of that tasty pemmican of yours." Old Bill glanced at Zach. "What are you waitin' for, boy? I told you to collect firewood. And get a lot of it. I aim to keep the fire going all night long."

From the old trapper's expression, Winona knew that he had something devious in mind in case Nate came. She absently went about making the meal, the whole time racking her brain for a way out of the predicament. Zach brought four loads of dead wood, which wasn't enough to suit Zeigler. He made Zach bring two more.

Old Bill walked to his horse and produced a coiled rope. Throwing it at Winona's feet, he said, "Now tie the brat's ankles so he won't try to sneak off."

It was senseless to argue when staring up the barrel of a heavy-caliber flintlock. Winona reluctantly did as she was bid, then resumed stirring the stew. Evelyn began to fuss, so Winona started to go to her. But she was stopped by a curt command.

"No you don't!" Old Bill said. "My stomach is more important than your sprout. Finish with my supper. Then you can rock her to sleep or whatever the hell you have to do."

Gloom gripped Winona's soul, a feeling that if she didn't act soon, she would lose those who meant more to her than life itself. Her husband and children were her reason for living.

Winona tested the broth with her fingertip. It was nearly done. She glanced at Old Bill, who was staring glumly at Evelyn as if he was of half a mind to shoot her.

Zachary also noticed and automatically tried to take the mountain man's mind off his sibling. "So how many folks have you killed over the years, Mr. Zeigler?"

"What's it to you?" Old Bill asked.

"I'd just like to know if the stories are true," Zach said.

"Live to be my age and you'll learn there's always a kernel of truth behind every tale," Old Bill said. He sank onto the ground and leaned against the log, the rifle draped across his thighs. "I reckon I've killed thirty people or thereabouts. Not countin' Injuns."

"Killed them how? Did you eat them?"

Old Bill laughed. "You keep harking back to those rumors about my being a cannibal. How come? Are you afeared I'm liable to plunk you in a pot and boil you alive?"

"I'm just curious," Zach said, glad that the old killer had taken his eyes off of Evelyn.

"Ain't you ever heard about what curiosity did to the cat?" Zeigler said. "A person should never go pokin' his nose in where it doesn't belong. Someone might up and lop it off."

The stew had come to a boil. Winona dipped the ladle in and tasted it. Her stomach was so empty it growled, but she ignored the pang. Using a small cloth, she gripped the metal handle and went to carry the pot over to Zeigler. Once she was close enough, she intended to toss the contents in his face, wrestle the rifle from his grasp, and shoot him between the eyes.

"What the hell do you think you're doin'?" Old Bill said. "Just leave the pot there and fill a bowl. It's not like we're at one of those fancy inns where they serve your food in bed."

Winona had no idea what he meant, but she

offered no objection. To rush him would prove fatal; all he had to do was lift his rifle and squeeze the trigger. She rummaged in a parfleche for a wooden bowl, filled it full to the brim, and carried it over in both hands. It was in her mind to hurl the contents into his eyes. As if he guessed, he squinted at her and elevated the rifle in her direction. She had no choice but to gently deposit the bowl beside him, then back away.

"Smart squaw," Old Bill said. "You'd be pushing up grass tomorrow if you'd done as you wanted."

Winona indicated the cradleboard. "May I hold my daughter now?"

"Suit yourself. Over there by the brat."

Bending, Winona scooped her hands under the cradleboard and was rising when Zeigler's foot lashed out, catching her in the shoulder. Knocked off balance, she fell to one knee and listened to his laughter.

"Ma, are you all right?" Zach cried.

"Of course she is, sonny," Old Bill said before she could. "A little tap like that won't bother no squaw. She's used to being slapped around by her men."

Zach was livid. "My pa has never laid a finger on my ma."

"Don't blame me if he's weak kneed. The only way to keep a woman in line is to beat her whenever she acts uppity. I know because I had a few wives in my younger days. Wasn't a one of them who didn't give me sass, but only once." Zeigler spooned soup into his mouth, then spoke while chewing. "Your pa could do with some lessons in how to handle women."

Winona held her hand out when her son opened his mouth to reply. She feared Zach would antagonize the mountain man into shooting. "I will get your soup."

"I'm not hungry, Ma."

"You will eat anyway. You must keep your strength up." Winona filled bowls for both of them. Although she had no real desire to eat, she did so to set an example for her offspring, who, once he had tasted the stew, downed it with relish.

Winona attended to Evelyn next. It was Indian custom to wean children at a later age than was common among whites, and Evelyn was at that age. Winona fed her some soup after mashing the jerky to a soft consistency.

Old Bill polished off his supper slowly, cast the bowl down, and belched. "Not bad, squaw," he said. "I have half a mind to keep you around just so you can fix me fine vittles every day. But we both know that wouldn't be too bright, would it? You'd gut me the first chance you got, wouldn't you?"

Winona knew better than to answer.

"That's all right. Don't say a word. The truth speaks for itself." Old Bill settled back. "Well, now that the eats are out of the way, I want you to tie your boy's wrists nice and tight. And I mean nice and tight. I'll be checking, so don't try to trick me."

The fleeting panic in Zach's eyes tugged at Winona's heart, but she had to do as bidden. Besides, something told her that Zeigler was in no great hurry to kill them. He might even wait until they reached his dugout. Covered by his rifle, she secured her son's arms. "I am sorry, Stalking Coyote," she whispered. "Do not give up hope."

Old Bill stood. "Now I want you to take that last piece of rope and tie your own ankles together."

Once more Winona obeyed. The mountain man walked toward her and she quickly pressed Evelyn to her bosom. Old Bill merely tested the knots, did the same with Zach, and nodded.

"You did a right fine job. Both of you lie on your sides."

Afraid that she had made a dreadful mistake and that Zeigler was about to abuse them or worse, Winona sank down, but balled her fists to strike when he came close enough. Zach was also coiled.

"Wouldn't want you to catch your death," Old Bill said. From their supplies he obtained two blankets. "These will keep you nice and warm until morning."

Winona lay still as Zeigler spread the blanket over her from her neck down. She noticed that he took particular care to tuck the edges under her feet. His intent was plain. He wasn't concerned about their comfort so much as he was about concealing the fact they were bound. To anyone surveying the camp, it would appear they were sleeping soundly.

Old Bill covered Zach, then straigthened up. "There, now. If you pa shows, he won't suspect a thing." He jabbed the boy with his rifle. "Don't try to throw the blanket off, brat. I'll be watching you the whole time."

Mother and son lay there and watched their captor tramp off into the undergrowth near the trail of tracks they had left. The fire crackled and snapped, casting light to the trees but no farther.

"Ma," Zach whispered. "What are we going to do? Pa will ride right into the buzzard's trap."

"I might be able to free my ankles without Zeigler noticing," Winona said, "but I will not escape without you. Do you think you can loosen your bounds?"

"I'll try my darnedest."

Many minutes passed. Winona waited as her son grunted and squirmed, and at length he gave a deep sigh.

"I'm sorry, Ma. I've tried my best, but all I've done is rubbed the skin off my wrists and gotten my arms all bloody."

"Then one of us must stay awake at all times. And when we hear your father coming, we must cry out to warn him."

Zachary frowned. He was upset that he had allowed himself to be trussed up, even more upset that he hadn't thought of a way of turning the tables on the sly old fox who had abducted them. "You can sleep first, if you want. I'm not very tired."

"Wake me when you can no longer keep your eyes open," Winona said. Making herself comfortable, with Evelyn tucked at her waist, she tried to relax so she could doze off. She didn't think she would be able to, not with Zeigler lurking out there somewhere, watching them, but her exhaustion and the comforting crackle of the fire lulled her to sleep.

Unknown to Winona King, another set of eyes was fixed on her as she fell asleep—a dark, stony set that belonged to Brule the Blood.

Brule had caught up with the travelers an hour before sunset and dogged their footsteps until they camped. It had been his intention to slay the white man, the boy, and the small girl at the first opportunity, then to have his way with the Shoshone. But it had soon become apparent that something was amiss. The white man made it a point to always hold a rifle on the others. By the actions and expressions of the woman and the boy, Brule discerned that they were being held captive. His insight was proven to be right when they were bound.

Brule did not know what to make of it. This was a new experience, and he resolved to study the situation to learn why the old trapper had taken the woman and children prisoner.

The mystery was compounded because the tracks told Brule that the white-eye, the Shoshone, and the breeds were all part of a party that had trailed Lassiter's bunch northward for quite a few sleeps. Two men in that party had gone on ahead; they were the ones who had fought at the grade and then hid from him in that gully.

How did the woman and children fit into the scheme of things? Was she the wife of one of the whites? Or had she been held at gunpoint the whole time, forced to ride along whether she wanted to or not? And why had the old trapper gone to hide in the brush near the trail? Was the trapper expecting the other two to show?

There were so many questions, and Brule was unable to answer a single one. He wanted to solve the mystery. So, for a while, he would content himself with shadowing them. Perhaps he would learn the answers.

Brule leaned back against a tree trunk, folded his arms, and permitted himself to doze off. Every now and then he would snap awake to look and listen. He saw the boy keeping watch and, later, the mother. Of the old trapper there was no sign, but Brule knew exactly where the man was concealed and could have slit the man's throat whenever he wanted.

A pink band framed the eastern sky when Brule roused himself and crept 100 yards along the creek to quench his thirst. He was hungry, but suppressed the need. There would be plenty of time to eat later. He hurried back.

The old white-eye had returned to the camp. The Shoshone was untying herself. Soon she had the boy untied too. While the boy fed limbs to the fire, the woman busied herself making breakfast.

Brule found it hard to maintain his self-control while they ate handfuls of pemmican and drank cups of coffee.

Shortly after sunrise they were mounted and bearing to the south once again, the old one bringing up the rear as before. Frequently the white man glanced over his shoulder as if expecting pursuit.

Traveling on a parallel course, Brule had no difficulty keeping them in sight. They rode no faster than a brisk walk. At midday they stopped briefly to water their animals and munch jerky. The woman breast-fed her daughter, and Brule imagined what it would be like to take the little one's place.

By late afternoon they were among rolling foothills. Beyond loomed sawtooth ridges and high, jagged spires. They climbed steadily until it was almost dark.

Brule had learned nothing all day. He was growing tired of their plodding rate of travel and debated whether to finish the white man off before it grew too dark. Either that or he had to go in search of food to tide him over until morning.

Deciding there was all the food he needed in their camp, Brule placed a hand on the hilt of his wonderful new knife and began to rise. Then he stopped because the most remarkable thing happened.

Winona King had made up her mind to break free of Zeigler's grasp, no matter what. She was convinced that as each day took them farther and farther away from Nate, so too did each day increase the chances that she or her children would be harmed.

During the afternoon Winona had contrived to whisper to Zach, but was thwarted when Old Bill refused to let them ride close to one another.

On a belt of grassy land halfway up the side of a ridge, Zeigler called a halt for the day. A small spring was nestled under a short rock overhang that bordered the grass. Here Winona watered the horses under the mountain man's hawkish gaze while Zach gathered wood.

Old Bill sat perched on a waist-high boulder, scratching himself, as Winona tethered the animals. Out of the corner of her eye she saw that he couldn't take his eyes off her, that her every movement came under close scrutiny. So it came as no surprise when he cleared his throat.

"You're a fine figure of a woman, Shoshone, if I do say myself."

"My husband will be glad to hear that you think he has good taste," Winona said.

Zeigler snorted. "It would be best for you to forget you ever met him. Nate King ain't your man anymore. I am."

"I am Grizzly Killer's forever," Winona said with a toss of her head. "I will never lie with another man. If he were to die, I would never take another husband."

"It's not like you have any choice," Old Bill said. "What I want, I take. And I want you." He strode toward her, leering.

Winona sensed the moment of truth had arrived. She was thankful that little Evelyn was yards away, propped in the cradleboard against a boulder. Squarely facing Zeigler, she said, "No man has the right to force himself on a woman. I will not let you put your hands on me."

"Ask me if I care about how you feel?" Old Bill said. Halting, he leveled his rifle. "I think I'd like to see how you look without that buckskin dress on. Take it off."

"Never."

Old Bill swiveled so his gun was fixed on Evelyn. "The dress or your daughter? Which will it be?"

"You are a despicable man," Winona said, backing slowly away. She cast about for a weapon—a rock, a club, anything. But there was nothing.

"Despicable?" Old Bill said. "Mercy me. Your husband has taught you better English than I use myself. Do you squeal in English?"

"Squeal?"

"You know," Zeigler said, his eyes straying to a point below her waist. "I sure do like it when a female squeals. Sets my blood to boilin'."

Winona suddenly bumped into one of the horses. She stopped and looked to the right and left, ready to bolt if he came one step nearer. The distinct click of the rifle hammer rooted her in place.

"I'm not playin' any games," Old Bill said, taking a bead on the cradleboard. "Either start strippin' to your birthday suit or you can kiss your bundle of joy good-bye."

Winona felt her mouth go dry. She had nowhere to run, no way to fight, even if her daughter's life wasn't at stake. "Do not hurt my child," she said.

"Then don't keep me waitin', damn it."

Desperate to avoid the inevitable, Winona reached up and fiddled with the neck of her dress, pretending to be loosening the strings of beads that encircled her throat. In reality, the only way for her to undress was to pull the buckskin garment up over her head.

Old Bill had the feral air of a wild cat about to swallow a minnow. He licked his lips and grinned wickedly, feasting on her turmoil. "It's been too long since last I had me a woman," he said. "Please me and I just might keep you alive so you can service me on a regular basis. What do you say?"

"I would rather be choked to death," Winona said before she could stop herself.

"That can be arranged, bitch," Old Bill said. "Hurry it the hell up!"

Despair tearing at her, Winona bent down to

grip her dress. Abruptly, past the mountain man, a small figure moved into sight. It was Zach, with a thick length of branch in both hands. Her son whipped the branch overhead as he charged and let out with a Shoshone war whoop.

For a man well into his sixties, Bill Zeigler had the reflexes of a 20 year old. He spun at the first note of the outcry, his rifle pointing at the boy's midsection.

"No!" Winona said, and flew at the mountain man like a tiger gone berserk, her fingers formed into claws to rake his face and eyes.

Old Bill glanced at her, realized she couldn't reach him before he could shoot, and faced Zach again. He expected Zach to swing the club. He figured he had plenty of time to kill the sprout and deal with the squaw. He was wrong.

Zachary King had learned to fight from a man whose survival skills were unsurpassed. His father had bested grizzlies, wolverines, painters, wolves, bobcats, hostiles, and renegade whites. With gun, knife, and tomahawk, Nate King was extremely skilled, and he had diligently tried to pass on some of that prowess to his son.

Even more importantly, Nate had seen fit to teach his son about unarmed combat—how to use his fists and feet as white men did, how to grapple and wrestle as Indians did.

If there was any one point Nate had stressed the most, it was always to do the unexpected. A close second had been that when Zach found his life hanging in the balance, he had to do whatever it took to win.

So as Zachary King hurled himself at Old Bill Zeigler, he did the last thing the mountain man would ever have anticipated. Instead of striving to bludgeon a man bigger and stronger than him, Zachary took deliberate aim and threw the club with all his might.

At that very instant, the rifle blasted.

Chapter Twelve

Nate King was fording the shallow river when shots rang out to the west, punctuated by screams of mortal terror. Jabbing his heels into the flanks of the stallion, he galloped up onto the bank and on into the cottonwoods. Once again his pistols were wedged under his belt. The loaded Hawken was in his left hand.

Jeremiah Sawyer had deserved a proper burial. Nate had delayed his pursuit of the cutthroats long enough to dig a grave deep enough to insure scavengers wouldn't unearth the body later. As a crowning touch he had added a crude cross fashioned from a broken branch, using whangs from his buckskin shirt to bind the pieces at the right angle.

Then Nate had climbed on the stallion and headed across the river to see if he could pick up the trail of Lassiter's gang before it was too dark.

Now, racing through the woodland, ducking branches and weaving among trunks, Nate recalled the recently made wagon tracks and feared for the safety of the poor pilgrims bound for the Oregon Country. Lassiter would give them the same treatment as Jeremiah.

Nate couldn't allow that to happen. He had covered over a quarter of a mile and was scouring the west side of the valley for the killers when he came upon a small knoll. Going up and over rather than around, he was shocked to see five horses tethered below and a giant of a man in the act of untying them.

There was no doubt as to whether it was a member of Lassiter's bunch. Immediately on seeing Nate, the giant tried to bring a rifle into play.

Streaking down the knoll, Nate was beside the man in a flash. He should have shot then and there. But he had the notion to take the giant alive in order to get certain questions answered. So he drove the stock of his Hawken against the giant's skull. It was like striking an anvil.

The man bellowed in pain and staggered, but didn't go down. Nate wheeled the stallion and closed in to deliver another blow. The giant had dropped his own rifle and appeared defenseless. Nate should have known better.

Whipping around, the giant swung his mallet of a fist, clipping the stallion on the point of its chin. A punch from a normal man would hardly have fazed it. This man stopped the horse in its tracks. Wobbly legs swaying, the stallion almost went down.

Nate raised the Hawken to swing again. The giant, moving with astonishing speed for a man of his bulk, leaped and grabbed hold of the front of Nate's shirt. The next moment Nate sailed over the head of his horse and crashed down on his stomach in the high grass.

Woozy from the impact, Nate tried to stand and turn. He was only halfway erect when fingers gouged into his shoulders and he was flung a dozen feet against the knoll. In the bargain he lost the Hawken. Dazed and winded, Nate twisted and saw the giant lumber toward him.

"Any last words, you son of a bitch, before I snap your spine like a dry twig?"

Nate kept his breath for saving his life. The giant lunged at him and he scrambled aside, then pushed upright. His right hand fell on a pistol and he drew, his arm a blur. Yet as fast as he was, the giant was faster.

Arms like coiled bands of steel closed around Nate. He was hoisted off the ground and found himself nose to nose with the puffing giant, who grinned and squeezed.

"I'm fixing to crush you, mister!"

Nate didn't doubt it. Shakespeare McNair had once told him about large snakes in Asia or Africa that crushed prey in mighty coils, and it seemed to him that he was about to suffer a similar fate. He surged against the man's arms, but as powerful as he was, he couldn't budge them.

The giant laughed and a lancing spasm racked Nate's chest. Then another. He was unable to take a deep breath and swore his ribs were about to collapse, splintered into fragments.

Nate couldn't use his arms or hands. His feet dangled uselessly and he couldn't get a grip on his weapons. The giant smirked, sensing victory.

And that was when Nate drove his forehead into his foe's nose. Cartilage crunched, blood sprayed, and a moment later, Nate was free.

The giant tottered backward, a hand covering his shattered nostrils. He acted more shocked than hurt.

To give the human bear a moment's respite was to invite disaster. Nate took two steps and dived. His arms looped around the giant's ankles. He heaved, felt the man's legs start to give, and heaved again. The smash of the heavy body hitting the earth was like that of a felled tree.

Nate rolled to the left, out of the giant's grasping reach. He was upright first and waded in with fists flying. A right hook caught the giant on the jaw, but did nothing more than make him blink.

Rumbling deep in his chest, the huge man sprang, swatting Nate's left jab aside. Again those massive arms coiled around Nate and lifted him into the air.

"You die!"

Spit and blood splattered Nate's face. He tried to slam his head against the giant's mouth but the man was prepared and jerked away.

"Not this time, bastard!"

Undaunted, Nate tried another tack; he rammed his knee into his adversary's groin, not once but three times in swift succession.

Sputtering, the giant released his hold and shambled off to the left, his enormous hands spread protectively over his privates.

Nate drew his tomahawk. He no longer cared about taking the man alive. Darting forward, he slashed at the giant's neck but the killer sprang out of harm's way and flourished a long knife, which he waved in tiny circles.

"It takes more than you've got to rub me out."

The Shoshones believed that warriors should never talk in the heat of battle, a belief shared by Apaches and others. Talking distracted men at crucial moments. It was considered the hallmark of poor fighters. Yet this man, gabby as he was, had proven to be as masterful a fighter as Nate had ever encountered.

Circling, Nate sought an opening. He had to be wary of the giant's greater reach and strength. Twice he feinted, but was unable to pierce the other's guard. The tomahawk and knife rang together like small bells, clanging with each strike.

Blood seeped from the giant's smashed nose into his mouth and he kept spitting it out to one side. Nate watched closely, his legs coiled like springs, and when the giant spat again, he dove, aiming a vicious swipe that would have ripped a thigh wide open. But the giant slid to the left with the agility of a mountain sheep.

The strain of all Nate had been through began to take its toll. His head ached abominably from the clout Jeremiah had given him, and his aching lungs strained to catch a breath. He had to end the fight quickly or the giant would end it for him.

As if sensing Nate's weakness, the huge man stalked in for the kill, swinging the knife like a sword, slashing high and low, seeking to penetrate Nate's guard. Nate retreated under the onslaught, parrying furiously, his fatigue rendering the heavy tomahawk more unwieldy than it would ordinarily be.

Having to focus on the giant to the exclusion of

all else, Nate had no idea what was behind him as he retreated step by hasty step. He suspected he was being forced back toward the forest. Confirmation came when tree limbs appeared overhead. Moments later he backed into a bole.

Evidently the giant had been waiting for that to happen. Snarling like an animal, he lanced his knife forward, seeking to pin Nate against the trunk. Nate wrenched aside, but not quickly enough. He nearly cried out as the keen blade sliced through his shirt and skin, drawing blood.

Skipping to the right, Nate crouched to meet the next attack. The wound was shallow but it stung like 1,000 bee stings at once.

The giant slowly turned. Wearing a mocking smile, he advanced, his arms constantly in motion as he flipped the knife from one hand to the other. His strategy was transparent. He would keep Nate guessing until the very last instant, then finish Nate off with a swift stroke.

That wasn't going to happen. Nate knew the giant expected him to keep on defending himself with the tomahawk, knew that the very last act the giant would expect was for him to snap back his arm and hurl the tomahawk in an overhand toss, yet that was exactly what he did. And he also knew, even as the smooth haft sped from his fingers, that the giant would easily dodge the tomahawk or deflect it. The latter proved to be the case.

Then, at the exact moment that the giant's knife arm was bent halfway around his body from the swing, Nate sprang, drawing his own blade as he did.

The giant's eyes widened to the size of walnuts

and he desperately tried to cover himself with his other arm.

Nate reached him first. Or rather, the knife did. It sank neatly between two of the giant's ribs, ripping through flesh and muscle with astounding ease, all the way to the hilt. Nate twisted, holding on tight as the giant tried to back out of reach. The man grunted, streaked his knife arm overhead, then stiffened, gasped, and melted as if made of soft wax.

Leaping back in case the giant tried to nail him while falling, Nate held his dripping blade at waist level. He was eager to finish his enemy off, but there was no need.

With a puzzled expression on his face, the giant eased onto his buttocks and sat there with a hand over the wound. He blinked and looked at Nate. "Damn. Never figured a runt like you would be the one—" Breaking off, he stiffened, then sagged onto his back.

Nate stepped nearer, prepared for any tricks.

"I want," the giant said weakly. "I want—"

"What?" Nate finally spoke, but he was destined to never know since the man expired with a drawn, strangled breath and went limp.

Nate took a deep breath to steady his racing pulse. He had been in more violent clashes than he cared to think about since settling in the Rockies, but few adversaries had pressed him as hard as the giant. "Whoever you were," he said softly, "you were as tough as they come."

The nicker of a horse reminded Nate there were more cutthroats abroad in the night. Shaking his head to clear his thoughts, he hastened to the animals. The stallion was grazing. The other five horses looked at him, but made no move to flee.

First Nate rounded up the two rifles. It turned out the giant had also owned a Hawken, the same caliber as Nate's. He put it in his bedroll. Next, taking the lead rope in hand, he mounted the stallion and rode to the south even though the shots and screams had arisen to the west.

There was a reason. Nate figured that he had all of the horses belonging to Lassiter's band of bloodthirsty killers, and he wasn't about to let them get their hands on the animals. He rode several hundred feet, slipped from the saddle, and secured all six horses.

After making sure his guns were loaded, Nate ran west. It wasn't long before fingers of flame appeared in the night. They took on the size and shape of three campfires spaced about 30 feet from one another in the shape of a circle. The pilgrims, Nate guessed, since only greenhorns would bother to build three fires where one would suffice.

Slowing, Nate worked his way as silently as a Shoshone warrior to a large fallen log. Kneeling, he studied the layout of the camp and the figures moving about.

A tall man with his thumbs hooked in his belt was strutting about as if he owned the valley. It had to be Lassiter, Nate guessed. Nearby two hard-hewn characters in buckskins were covering a cluster of frightened pilgrims. A fourth killer was visible in one of the wagons, sorting through belongings in search of plunder.

Of the pilgrims, two were bawling women. A third female, younger and fairer of form, was glaring at Lassiter. A young man stood beside her, his hands in the air. Another man stood meekly next to a wagon wheel, three children grasping his legs in fear.

Nate shifted, then choked off an oath. Two bodies lay in spreading red pools—that of a man in homespun clothes and that of a small boy, a child no older than Zach.

"Even children," Nate whispered to himself, horrified. The sight chilled him to the bone. No matter how long he lived in the wilderness, no matter how much slaughter he beheld, he found it impossible to regard wanton butchery with anything other than total loathing. Some of his fellow trappers had no such qualms. To them, death was so common an occurrence that it hardly deserved a second thought. They could stare at heaps of bodies killed in a raid and not be moved in the least.

Not Nate. He burned with sheer rage on seeing the child. Only the worst sort of men could do such a thing, men with no morals, no scruples, no conscience. Men as hard as the mountains themselves. Men whose hearts had changed to stone.

The thought gave Nate pause. Was it proper to even call them men when they were more akin to the savage beasts that shared the land they roved? Anyone capable of shooting an innocent child in cold blood was the scum of the earth, despicable beyond redemption, as soulless as a grizzly or a fierce painter.

Nate raised the Hawken and extended it across the log, making it a point not to let the barrel scrape the rough bark. He tucked the stock to his shoulder and took precise aim at Lassiter.

According to Jeremiah Sawyer, Earl Lassiter was the brains of the bunch. Kill him and the rest would be thrown into fleeting panic, giving Nate the time he needed to pick them off one by one.

Without warning, Lassiter turned and stepped to the wagon being ransacked. The short man inside said something. Nodding, Lassiter climbed in.

Nate held his fire. He wanted a clear shot, and he only caught glimpses of the cutthroat leader as he moved about under the canvas.

One of the men guarding the pilgrims, a killer wearing a blue cap, reached out to stroke the young woman's hair. She recoiled and slapped his hand. In retaliation, the man smacked her with such force she stumbled back against a wagon, which spurred the young man beside her into lowering his arms and moving toward the killer.

Nate saw the man in the blue cap train his rifle on the husband. A wicked gleam lit the killer's visage. In another second he would fire, slaying the husband in front of the young wife's eyes.

Nate couldn't allow that. Swiveling, he glued the front bead to the killer's chest, lined up the rear sight with the bead, and stroked the trigger.

The man in the blue cap, unknown to Nate King, was Dixon. The lead ball tore into his chest, passed completely through a lung, and burst out his back between the shoulder blades. The impact lifted him off his feet and flung him to the grass, where he convulsed briefly, trying to marshal his fading willpower. The last sensation he experienced was that of a black hand enfolding all he was in its inky grip.

Ben Kingslow had been standing near Dixon when the shot shattered the night. Instantly he crouched and snapped return fire at a cloud of gunsmoke in the woods.

Nate King, already on the move, heard the ball smack into the top of a log and ricochet off. He darted into a thicket and bore to the left.

Inside the wagon, Earl Lassiter leaped up at the booming crack and jumped onto the front seat. The shot had come from in the trees, not in the camp. He saw Dixon down and dead and Ben Kingslow rapidly reloading. "How many? Where are they?" he shouted.

Kingslow had no idea and pivoted to say as much.

By then Nate had raced over 15 feet. His right hand flashed to a pistol and it cleared leather in a practiced draw. One handed, he sighted at the killer who was reloading, then fired, rushing his shot.

This time Nate's aim was off. Kingslow was in the act of pulling his ramrod out when the shot caught him high on the temple. It was like being pounded by a hammer. The next he knew, he was lying on his back, stunned, his rifle no longer in his hands. He groped for it, rising onto his elbows.

Of the pilgrims, Katie Brandt was first to regain her senses after being startled by the gunfire. Belatedly she realized that whoever was out there was trying to help them. One of their captors was dead, another severely wounded. They would never have a better opportunity to turn the tide.

"Glen! Bob!" Katie shouted. "We have to help!"

Kingslow was almost to his knees when a hell-cat in the guise of a young woman flew into him, her nails raking his cheek and neck. He tried to shove her away but Glen Brandt was on him a heartbeat later, slamming fists into his face and head. Kingslow grabbed for his knife, felt his wrist grabbed in turn as the knife came clear.

Glen saw his wife seize the killer's wrist and leaped to her aid, adding his hands to hers. Both of them bent and shoved upward simultaneously, shearing the blade deep into the cutthroat's stomach at a 90-degree angle.

All this while, Nate had continued circling, hoping for a clear shot at Lassiter. Suddenly the leader and the short man spilled from the wagon and sprinted into the cottonwoods.

Of Nate's three guns, only one pistol was still loaded, which didn't stop him from speeding in pursuit of the renegades. He bounded past a tree and saw the short killer ten feet off, fleeing.

Snip sensed someone was behind him and whirled. He fired from the hip, and had he been a shade steadier, he would have put a ball through his pursuer's gut.

But as it was, Snip missed, and Nate immediately pointed his pistol and fired. At that range, the .55-caliber had the wallop of a cannon. Snip's head dissolved in a geyser of brains and gore.

That left only Earl Lassiter, who fled through the forest as if demons were on his trail. He'd glanced back in time to see Snip meet his Maker. The glimpse he had of the big man who was after them was sufficient to tell him who it was: Nate King, a close friend of Shakespeare McNair's and

Jim Bridger's. He knew King was a free trapper whose reputation for honesty and courage was unmatched by any save the other two living legends.

Nate King! Lassiter fumed as he fled. Of all the cursed luck! He couldn't understand how King had learned of his band. Then he recollected seeing Jeremiah Sawyer and King together at a rendezvous. There had to be a connection, and Lassiter would ponder it later. For now he had his hide to save.

All his guns empty, Nate sped in the killer's wake. He pulled his knife and reversed his grip.

Lassiter was running flat out, glancing back every few yards. The next time he did, he neglected to check the ground in front of him first.

Nate saw the murky outline of a small boulder. He poured on the speed as Lassiter tripped and sprawled forward. Lassiter landed on his hands and knees, and like a coiling serpent he spun around and began to jerk up his rifle. By then Nate was less than eight feet away. His supple body flowed into a smooth, superbly coordinated throw. The butcher knife cleaved the air straight and true.

Earl Lassiter's final sight was of a dully glittering blade as it thudded into his chest.

Chapter Thirteen

It was Zachary King's hurling of the club that saved his life. As he threw, he naturally shifted his body into the direction of the throw. The slight movement was just enough to throw Old Bill Zeigler's aim off.

The bullet missed Zach by a hair. He never slowed his charge, and he was on Old Bill a second before his mother. The mountain man roared and snapped his rifle on high. But between Zach and Winona, they brought him crashing to the earth.

Winona fought in a frantic frenzy for the lives of her children. She gouged her nails into Old Bill's right eye as he tried to elbow her in the face. His howl was fearsome. She saw him let go of the rifle and grasp the hilt of his knife. To stop him from using it, she clamped her hands on his forearm and held fast. "Zach! Get his pistol!" she cried.

Young Zach spotted the butt jutting from the top of Old Bill's belt. He made a grab for it, but was given a swat that sent him tumbling and set his ears to ringing. When he pushed to his feet, he was terrified to find Old Bill on top of his mother, choking the life from her with one hand while striving to pull his knife with the other.

Winona tossed and bucked, trying to dislodge the demented mountaineer while simultaneously attempting to prevent him from unlimbering his blade.

In a twinkling Zach rushed to help her. Balling his fists, he barreled into Zeigler and delivered a flurry of blows that would have rendered the older man senseless if Zach had been a few years older. As it was, all he succeeded in doing was drawing Old Bill's wrath.

Zeigler's rage was such that he no longer entertained the notion of keeping mother or son alive. They had hurt him badly, and for that they were both going to die. He cuffed the boy, knocking him to his knees, then clasped both hands around the mother's slender neck.

In a moment of panic Winona grasped his wrists and urgently tried to pry the man's hands from her windpipe. She was so concerned about being strangled that she forgot all else.

Not so with Zach. He had the presence of mind to remember the pistol and knife. Diving at Zeigler's waist, he pretended to snatch at the pistol with one hand and when Old Bill lowered an arm to block him, he seized the knife instead.

Old Bill didn't feel the blade slide from its sheath. He did feel a strange tingling in his innards though, and he looked down to discover seven inches of cold steel planted in his abdomen. Wailing like a banshee, he leaped to his feet. As he did, Zach ripped the knife loose.

"Damn your bones!" Old Bill said, staggering backward. He told himself that this couldn't be happening to him, that a brat and a miserable woman couldn't be getting the better of him. He tried to stop the crimson spray shooting from his ruptured gut, but it was like trying to plug a cracked dam. Looking up, he sought his rifle, but Winona King held it.

"Oh, no," Old Bill said and clawed at his pistol.

"Oh, yes," Winona said. She shot him in the face.

The lanky frame of the grizzled madman did a slow pirouette to the ground. It wound up on its back, blank eyes fixed on the heavens.

Zach stared at the neat hole in Zeigler's forehead. The thought of how close they had come to dying caused a tiny shudder to ripple down his back. "We did it," he said numbly. "We're safe now."

Stepping over to him, Winona draped an arm across his shoulders. "Yes, we are," she said, struggling to catch her breath after her ordeal. "Tomorrow at first light we will head north to rejoin your father."

"He should have been back by now, shouldn't he?" Zach asked.

Winona thought so, but she wanted to spare her son any more anguish than they had already been through. "I would guess that he is busy tracking down the men we were after. There is no need to worry about him. Your father can take care of himself better than any man I know."

"That's why he's the best there is at what he does," Zach said proudly. Remembering the knife in his hand, he squatted to wipe the blade clean on the grass. Behind him there was the barest whisper of movement, so faint that he thought it was the wind, that the breeze had picked up, and he turned to let the cool air fan his face.

Eight feet away stood a swarthy warrior holding a rifle leveled in their direction.

"Ma!" Zach exclaimed, bouncing erect.

Winona whirled, bewildered by her son's outcry since the danger was past. Then she set eyes on the warrior and knew by the style of his hair that he was a Blood. "Get behind me," she said, remembering that Jeremiah Sawyer had told them about a certain Blood who rode with Earl Lassiter. It was too much of a coincidence not to be the same person.

"I'll protect you, Ma," Zach said, moving in front of her.

Grabbing her son's arm, Winona swung him around to her rear. The Blood regarded them with a hint of amusement and something else. He took a step, then gestured curtly for her to drop the rifle. It was empty anyway, so she did.

Brule the Blood had seen the white man slain. He had admired the woman's fierce resistance, which made her all the more desirable since Blood men looked for fighting spirit in their women. Being fully aware of her battle prowess, he was not about to give her the chance to do to him as she had done to the white man. Keeping her covered, he took several strides.

Winona tried a bluff to buy time. "Who are